Decree
of
the Watchers

Decree of the Watchers

Verdict from Another Dimension

RUBEN RIOS CEPERO

iUniverse®

DECREE OF THE WATCHERS
VERDICT FROM ANOTHER DIMENSION

iUniverse books may be ordered through booksellers or by contacting:

iUniverse
1663 Liberty Drive
Bloomington, IN 47403
www.iuniverse.com
1-800-Authors (1-800-288-4677)

Because of the dynamic nature of the Internet, any web addresses or links contained in this book may have changed since publication and may no longer be valid. The views expressed in this work are solely those of the author and do not necessarily reflect the views of the publisher, and the publisher hereby disclaims any responsibility for them.

Any people depicted in stock imagery provided by Thinkstock are models, and such images are being used for illustrative purposes only.
Certain stock imagery © Thinkstock.

ISBN: 978-1-4917-8299-6 (sc)
ISBN: 978-1-5320-0392-9 (hc)
ISBN: 978-1-4917-8300-9 (e)

Library of Congress Control Number: 2015920008

Print information available on the last page.

iUniverse rev. date: 09/20/2017

Contents

Acknowledgements

As I journeyed through the dimension of the Watchers, I was blessed with the company of some incredible people. They included the team at IUniverse, who provided valuable guidance, outstanding content editing, and great input, and also had tremendous patience with me.

Several family members and friends helped me, in many different ways, to produce this book. Thank you for your love, your unwavering friendship, and never-ending encouragement. Thanks for patiently reading various iterations of the manuscript, for your honest constructive critiques, and for an incredible cover design.

And special thanks to my beloved grandniece Aminah for being a steadfast, though admittedly biased, fan and to my little granddaughter Sophia, who considers me the greatest grandpa in the entire planet, for her never-ending affection and for never failing to laugh at my silly humor.

May the Infinite Mind bless you all, keep you safe, smile upon you, and give you peace.

Dedicated to the memory of

Leslie Schmedes,

a great friend and mentor,

a special person who went about,

in quiet but powerful ways, affirming the

value of every person as a child of

the Infinite Mind.

Prologue

Despite my desperate attempts to avoid it, I realized I was going to crash with an eighteen-wheeler that had suddenly turned in front of my car with no warning. I didn't panic; my reactions were quick but intentional. However, after having tried three times to take evasive action, I knew I could not avoid broadsiding the truck. I also knew the chances of surviving that accident were slim and that it could result in my death.

Suddenly, another stunning realization occurred to me: it no longer seemed that my death in that accident was an avoidable possibility; I felt absolutely certain I *was* going to be killed that evening. I always knew, that is, academically, that I would die one day, just as everyone else, but I never thought it would be in a violent accident.

This thought was followed immediately by a feeling of regret that my family would receive a call with tragic news that night. Then, in a fraction of a moment that seemed unreal; eerily long, yet too short for me to take any effective action, I heard an ear-shattering noise and felt my body jolted by an incredibly powerful force. My car crashed into the truck and the front end went under the truck's cab. *I guess this is how I'm going to die,* I thought. The airbag detonated so quickly that I wasn't even aware of it happening. My hands were jerked off the steering wheel violently. One hand became swollen almost instantly.

In that seemingly long moment, the truck's tires rolled over and crushed the driver's side of my car as well as both my legs. Then came what I feared most - a massive explosion. At age forty-nine, I died engulfed in flames; burned beyond recognition. My family received the call.

* * * * * *

However, in another dimension, these events had been foreseen. It had been decreed that they were to be altered and they were.

* * * * * *

A moment after the crash, I realized I was alive but trapped under the cab of a truck in the middle of a busy intersection during rush hour. My front and rear windshields had shattered. The car became so filled with smoke that I couldn't see a thing through any of the windows. The detonated airbags and much of the driver's side of the car now pressed against and greatly constricted me. I did not have the leverage I needed to open the driver's side door. I tried opening it, but it seemed hopelessly stuck and refused to budge. Since my right hand was already in a lot of pain, I was able to use only my left hand, but, it was not strong enough to push open the door. I began to fear that, at any moment, the car might explode in flames and tried again to force the door open, this time adding my knee to the effort. Finally, the door creaked open, but just enough to allow me to struggle out of the car. Not being able to see out of any of the car's windows, I had no idea what I would be walking into. I feared that, after surviving a horrific crash, I might be struck by an oncoming vehicle while trying to escape a possible car fire. But, I figured my chances of survival were probably better out of the car than in it, so I got out as quickly as possible.

I walked away from that accident with an injured hand. However, since my head and face were covered in blood from superficial scrapes, I was taken to a hospital emergency room and kept under observation for several hours. The police officer on the scene came to see me at the hospital. Standing at my bedside, he uttered some strange words that one would not normally expect to hear from a police officer investigating an accident. He said, "The angels were with you tonight."

I didn't realize then just how significant those words were and how deeply they would settle in my mind. Since infancy, I'd had a number of close encounters, but always seemed to miss my appointment with horrible injury or premature death. Once, during a particularly challenging time in my life, memories of various traumatic events flooded my mind. They came in rapid succession and sharp detail, but not in a negative way. As I thought about those events that morning, I had an unexpected insight. Despite enduring a great deal of emotional pain, resulting from poverty, abuse, and abandonment in a profoundly dysfunctional family, it seemed that I had been watched and supernaturally protected several times from horrible injury or violent death. I started pondering various questions: *Was I supernaturally protected and, if so, why? Is there a special purpose or destiny being worked out in my life that I have yet to fulfill?*

Curiously, around the same time, I had started wondering about the size of the universe. It seemed to me that, somehow, this was directly related to the other questions I was pondering. It has been said, by those who spend much of their lives studying such things, that if we were to travel at the speed of light, or roughly 5.9 trillion miles per year, it would take about 93 billion years to go from one edge of the observable universe to the other. Within that incredibly enormous expanse, which is infinitely greater than what the human mind can imagine, there are hundreds of billions of galaxies, each with hundreds of billions of stars and innumerable mysteries. Outside the observable universe is what I call the Great Beyond. What lies there has not been seen by human eyes and cannot yet be detected even by our most advanced instruments. This begs the question: *What significance can an individual human life have in the context of this vast universe and what may lie beyond it?*

From the dawn of history, we've pondered this and other related questions. Actually, all our philosophical musings about the purpose of life boil down to two fundamental questions: Is there any purpose to my life or are we mere accidents of nature experiencing an essentially meaningless, temporary organic existence? If there is purpose, what is it? We wonder even more about what purpose there could possibly be in the incomprehensible suffering endured by so many.

Long ago, writers from the Near East claimed that inter-dimensional beings intervened in human affairs to ensure the fulfillment of destinies designed for certain individuals or groups of people. These ancient writers seemed to believe that narratives were encoded, so to speak, in the universal space-time continuum, just as sound was once etched into vinyl records and as audiovisual messages are now embedded in digital storage media. Among these writings are accounts about a group of powerful inorganic beings known as the Watchers.

According to one account, the Watchers observed the severe oppression and near annihilation of a group of innocent and defenseless people - a horrendous event, before it had taken place at an undefined future time. In a mysterious timeless dimension, a court convened and rendered judgment in favor of the oppressed group. The court then issued a decree that immediately and permanently altered the course of future events.

Thousands of years after these accounts were recorded, a tribunal of these mysterious Watchers once again convened. They now rendered judgment over the life of one person, an ordinary, twenty-first-century man who as a child had suffered unspeakable abuse.

The Watchers observed this man throughout all of his life. They monitored, guided, and even altered events that would affect him -always with the intention of ensuring he had the opportunity to freely choose or reject a unique destiny that had been ordained for him. It was a destiny that was designed before his organic conception and transcended the limits of time, space, and his own physical existence.

Without ever infringing on his freedom, the Watchers gave meaning to this man's suffering, an ordeal which would otherwise have been painfully meaningless. They guarded his freedom, but not necessarily what is commonly perceived as freedom, such as the self-gratification often disguised as liberty or even the lack of repression. What they guarded was the man's ability to freely choose his path without the chains that often bind the human spirit. But when given the opportunity, what did he choose? How did he exercise that freedom?

Chapter 1

Guardians of Space-Time

Long ago, a race of organic beings found themselves on a planet near the center of the observable universe that was uniquely suited for them. The planet was located, along with several other planets, in a solar system nestled deep within a spiraling galaxy, which was one of many billions of galaxies. The planet, a beautiful blue sphere that shined like an iridescent jewel floating in the blackness of space, was known as Earth.

However, though everything needed for their well-being was on this planet, these unfortunate beings were not at peace. They were confined within the space time continuum along with a horde of evil non-organic entities who, after thoroughly blinding their eyes of reason and enslaving them, oppressed them mercilessly.

But, as they had little or no sensory perception of their captors, they were not even aware they had been taken captive. After many ages of nearly perpetual suffering, these beings, who were then known as humans, became convinced they were alone in the vastness of the universe and that their planet, a living orb teeming with life, came to its unique position in its star system by sheer accident. Many thought their planet was a cosmic orphan, wandering aimlessly through space. Nevertheless, they were not alone.

Since the beginning of time, Watchers were standing guard over the space-time continuum. They had a special interest in this unique planet and focused intently on the humans who inhabited it. During the humans' organic sojourn, before humanity entered the Infinite Realm, the Watchers served as their guardians. Watchers are extraordinarily intelligent and powerful beings who exercise near-supreme authority over the material universe and peer into every corner of the cosmos.

Though humans had studied and marveled at the mysteries, precision, and apparent design of the universe, they could not perceive the infinite intelligence that designed it and the Great Beyond that lies past the frontier of what they could observe or detect with their instruments. Neither could they perceive the Watchers, who are inorganic luminescent beings composed of pure energy and were, generally, invisible to organic beings. Only in rare instances did Watchers materialize and allow themselves to be seen by humans. At times, the Watchers' energy took on a mysterious appearance that seemed like flowing liquid color, brilliant light or extreme heat. Other times, they appeared as beings with audible and even palpable qualities.

The lives of the few people who ever encountered these beings were forever changed. Those privileged to have seen Watchers described the emanation of an incredible force, an aura that stimulated and energized their senses beyond what they had ever imagined possible. Some claimed to have experienced new dimensions of reality. What these people described was incomprehensible to other humans.

After encounters with these extra-dimensional beings, some of these otherwise ordinary humans developed a sensory awareness that transcended the natural spectrum of human perception. Some experienced emotions and feelings visually; seeing the colors of joy or passion. Others could taste the flavor of sound or hear the vibrancy of colors. At times, they inadvertently revealed their peculiar sensations to others through curious expressions such as "a brilliantly yellow joy" or "a crushing black pain."

They would occasionally muse aloud about the sound of a spectacularly beautiful golden sunset or the sweet flavor of harmonious music. Seeds of human inspiration and creativity grew out of the experiences of this select group of people, although they were often thought to be dim-witted or even insane.

The Watchers, along with many other beings, inhabit the Infinite Realm - a dimension unbound by time and space. Watchers appeared in many different forms. At times, they manifested themselves with a barely detectable, mostly transparent humanlike form, with a luminescent glow that seemed to be perpetually hovering. Some have no resemblance at all to human beings, but have the physical features of other organic earthly creatures. Some Watchers have a strangely metallic quality, similar in appearance to bronze or brass. Others have the appearance of embers glowing in extreme heat. The energy released by just one of these glowing beings could affect an entire planet. The mere sight of any of these beings always caused great fear in humans.

Although Watchers exist in a dimension outside the space-time continuum, when necessary, they entered the observable universe and the human realm as well. As agents of the Infinite Mind, the master architect of all realities, they were also able to alter the course of events on Earth from their own dimension.

There once lived a human on Earth, a man called Adam, who since his birth had been the target of and relentlessly stalked by an unseen enemy. The Adversary, prince of the Malevolence; the evil entities who held sway over the entire planet for many ages, was bent on Adam's destruction. He continually oppressed him and subjected him to profound suffering. Adam's spirit and mind had been hopelessly bound by the cruel Adversary and the Malevolence, who had stalked him nearly his entire life, just as they had his ancestors.

Unaware of the existence of the Malevolence, Adam had grown to believe that suffering was merely his lot in life. For as long as he could remember, he had been aware of a perpetual *wrongness* about himself that he didn't understand, something that came to define his very character and personality. Adam could not remember a time when this wrongness had not been part of him. Indeed, it *was* him—or so he felt.

3

The Adversary knew Adam well, down to his genetic code. He manipulated and exploited all of Adam's pain, insecurities, dysfunctions, and fears. The Adversary and his agents of evil toyed with Adam. They would lull him into complacency with a strange sense of security in his perpetual pain, then suddenly and mercilessly inflict excruciating torture on him; plunging him into distress.

Adam became accustomed to the effect of evil and the predictability of failure in his life. The Malevolence motivated endless rationalizations, excuses and justifications for every negative thought or reaction he entertained or engaged in as a response to the pain and abuse he had experienced. Eventually, Adam was reduced to a pitiful, self-loathing creature stuck in a cycle of self-destructive behavior.

The Malevolence met Adam every morning, before he had even gotten out of bed. Every dawn would awaken in him a dark depression that had, early in his life, settled deep within his soul. The evil entities followed Adam everywhere he went.

They rode the subway with him on his way to work, stalking his every step. Invading his mind, they whispered thoughts throughout the day. They were present at his family events and social gatherings with co-workers or acquaintances. Adam did not have one person he could call a friend and had no one to talk to about his ordeal.

The Malevolence would settle down with Adam every evening, and when Adam was finally asleep, would visit his dreams with interminable vexation. Every day and night, the Malevolence injected scathing self-criticism, condemnation, fear, and shame directly into Adam's mind in a concerted effort to coerce him into abhorring himself. Their mission was to cause Adam to self-destruct.

The Malevolence had attempted to end Adam's organic life several times. When he was only a few months old, the evil beings caused Adam to fall onto a concrete floor. Later, when he was a young boy, they attempted to use fire to destroy or permanently disfigure Adam.

Their efforts were thwarted by the Watchers. As a result, the Adversary resolved that, instead of killing Adam's organic body, they would destroy the essence of his being—his spirit and dignity.

Throughout much of his life, Adam remained unaware of the doings of the Malevolence in his life. The evil had infiltrated his mind at a very young age with skillfully disguised voices he thought were his own. The evil entities would take every opportunity to inject self-criticism of Adam's mistakes and character flaws; using a specific negative event—whether it was major or relatively insignificant made no difference. Once they had opened a valve to a well they had filled with self-hatred, they would stealthily blend their voices with Adam's internal voice.

He would soon find fault not just with everything he did, but with everything he was; his entire being. The Malevolence caused Adam to feel inferior to everyone else he knew or saw, however vile they might have been.

Eventually, Adam came to feel most people hated him for no reason other than that he was who he was. The Malevolence caused Adam to feel despised and to despise himself. Even the sound of his own name was repugnant to him.

Adam was intimately familiar with sorrow, one of his constant companions, along with shame and humiliation. He lived in the shadow of a dark cloud, perpetually dissatisfied with himself and sad about just being alive. His world was one of deep, dark valleys of emotional pain, with very few hills of joy and no peaks of elation. His pain penetrated to the depths of his soul, the result of abuse and a profoundly dysfunctional family life he endured as a child and young adult. Hopelessness was so palpable to him that it often made him feel sick to his stomach.

The Malevolence studied Adam intently, observing and memorizing his habits and even his minute physiological reactions to certain stimuli. The Watchers also closely observed this man and monitored every aspect of his life, from beyond a gate between the material world and the Infinite Realm. They had seen his suffering and his struggles and, without his knowledge, occasionally intervened on his behalf.

The Watchers, just as the Adversary did, knew every detail about Adam. The Watchers knew his strengths and weaknesses, his successes and failures. They knew his innermost hopes, dreams, and intentions, his mind and character, and even his genetic code. Indeed, the Watchers knew Adam while he was yet in the loins of his ancestors. All his unique traits had been foreseen long before his organic conception. Before the dawn of Earth-time, they had observed Adam and, having been entrusted with his destiny, had made provision for it.

The Watchers were to ensure he had an opportunity to freely choose or reject what had been planned for him ages before he had even been born. There came a time in which the Malevolence bore down so heavily on Adam that he was nearly crushed. Feeling almost hopeless, he considered surrendering and taking his own life. Alone in his apartment, Adam cried out in desperation. Despite having no certainty and even doubting that such an entity even existed or cared about his plight, he hoped that some all-powerful being or force would hear him, listen to his plea and care to act upon it.

"If you are real, please help me! Please help me. You're my only hope."

* * * * * *

However, this had been foreseen in the Infinite Realm. Intervention had already been ordained long before the inception of Adam's organic existence. The Realm had anticipated and heard his cry ages before it went out.

Chapter 2

A Cry Goes Out

"Sir, shall we intervene?"

Upon detection of an urgent signal from Earth, an attendant in the Infinite Realm approached an Elder of the Council of Watchers for authorization to act.

* * * * * * *

In desperation, the man known as Adam cried out for relief from excruciating anguish caused by an affliction that had tormented him nearly his entire organic life. Piercing the silence of a dark night, his cry went out from Earth, soaring through the universe and the Great Beyond as if it were a radio wave.

* * * * * * *

The signal reached the Infinite Realm where the Watchers had been anticipating it ages before Adam's birth.

During their organic sojourn, humans would often stare at the night sky, mesmerized by stars that had actually ceased to exist long before their forefathers walked the planet. At times, they were observing the birth of a star in a distant past; in a sense, seeing the beginning from the end. As agents of the Infinite Mind, who sees the end from the beginning, the Watchers observed the start, the progression and the intended culmination of Adam's suffering as clearly as if he were present in their own dimension.

With the customary calculated precision of the Watchers, the Elder replied, "We must first consider all possible ramifications."

Despite possessing incredible powers, the Watchers did not rush to intervene on Adam's behalf. Humans would have seen the Watchers' lack of an immediate response as cold scientific observation, much as they engaged in when they studied and experimented on lower earthly life forms. Humans understood how a compassionate doctor might have to temporarily ignore the cries of an injured child suffering in pain in order to render urgently needed treatment to save life or limb. But their organic nature often prevented them from transcending their individual temporal experiences and viewing their own suffering in the larger context of universal purposes.

Far from being dispassionate, the Watchers were fully invested in securing Adam's freedom to choose his destiny. However, they had to maintain a delicate balance. Interference with mankind's freedom of choice was strictly forbidden by the protocols of the Infinite Realm.

* * * * * * *

The Watchers were not the only inorganic beings interested in Adam's cry. The highly intelligent and powerful disembodied entities known as the Malevolence also detected and took great interest in it with intentions that were far from benevolent. These beings, though contained within the space-time continuum with humans, inhabited a dark domain not naturally perceptible by organic beings. Hence, most humans were totally unaware of their existence.

After Adam's cry went out from Earth, in a dimension known as the Dark Realm, the Prince of the Malevolence - man's ancient adversary, addressed his horde.

"The creature has petitioned the Infinite Realm for release."

One of his minions had the temerity to question his lord.

"How can he petition the Realm? He has no sensory perception of it and therefore does not actually know that it even exists. Humans believe only that which they can perceive with their physical senses. As far as he is concerned, the Realm is merely a myth, a children's story. His cry is a meaningless gasp of pain. The creature is our slave. The Realm cares nothing about him—he has been abandoned inside this wretched container of space and time!" Pleased with his keen insight, the minion laughed with delight.

The Adversary did not laugh, but, instead, erupted in rage at his servant's impudence.

"Stupid fool! The creature, my slave, has not been forgotten by the Realm. No conscious organic creature is ever forgotten by that detestable Realm."

"Why should we be concerned about this insignificant human? He poses no threat to us. He has made no impact on his world and no notable accomplishments that would affect our purposes."

Greatly irritated that the minion dared to persist in questioning his concerns, the Adversary growled.

"Is any link in a chain insignificant? Do you not recall that less than a mere one thousand Earth-years ago, a child named Martin, whom you also considered to be insignificant, became a man who changed the course of his world, leading many of those repulsive organic creatures out of our grasp? Was it not fewer than five hundred years later that another child with the same name inspired many of the humans in his nation and throughout this vile planet to take actions favorable to Realm?"

The Adversary knew full well, as most humans unfortunately did not, that each person was an integral link in a powerful chain, with incredible potential encoded in their DNA. He also knew that any human creature in whose temporal experiences the Infinite Realm displayed any interest had supreme importance, though he knew not what their particular destiny might be.

"The creature's petition has been registered by the tribunal," said the Malevolent Prince.

The Malevolent Prince exploded in a violent rage and inflicted a savage punishment upon his minion, casting him to the darkest regions of the observable universe. With a frightful howl, the minion disappeared deep into a black hole. The Adversary then turned his attention to the rest of his horde.

"The Infinite Mind believes he will prevail against me. It is true that we are limited by our containment in this insufferable prison of space and time. He controls and manipulates events for his perverse ends.

However, we still have some advantages, not the least of which is that which the Realm cherishes most: the so called, "freedom of choice". The Infinite Mind believes this freedom of choice is the greatest gift he has given to his pathetic organic creatures. With their inherently flawed nature and temporary existence, those foul creatures cannot resist immediate gratification of their temporal needs and desires. They have no true freedom."

The Adversary let out a derisive growling laugh.

"Add a good measure of suffering, and you have a formula for success. Our success! These creatures refuse to accept the limitations of their organic nature. Their aspirations always exceed their reach. These factors, combined with this so-called freedom, will be their undoing. When given the choice, with some coercion, these pathetic creatures invariably choose bondage and death over life and freedom."

In abject fear of their malevolent prince, his subjects groveled while crying out in a grating chorus, "How else may we serve you, Lord Prince?"

"There is nothing else you can do but continue to stalk and weaken him. I will seek an audience with the detestable tribunal to see if I might be able to expedite his demise."

* * * * * *

The Infinite Realm's perspective on freedom of choice is vastly different from that of the Malevolent Prince.

The Watcher further enlightened the attendant, "The well-being of conscious organic creatures depends more on realities they comprehend internally than on their external circumstances. It is not pain that most affects their sense of well-being and influences their ultimate success, but the absence of meaning. Every conscious being craves meaning. The Adversary believes the freedom granted to humans, combined with their flawed nature and the limitations of their temporal organic existence, will result in their destruction. He has erred. His error will be *his* undoing."

The attendant probed for more clarity.

"My Lord, is not the Man merely an organic creature with a temporary existence? The Adversary is engaged in intense efforts to destroy his species. Besides attempting to thwart or corrupt the Man's freedom of choice, the Adversary manipulates his flawed nature through his natural fear of death. Through his incessant oppression, he coerces the Man into choices that can potentially lead to his demise. How can he survive? And if he does survive, will he truly be able to choose the path of light above the dark path? Was not his ability to choose wisely impaired from his organic birth?"

The Watcher responded, "The Adversary is quite effective in manipulating the Man's defects. However, he does not realize that the combination of this freedom, the Man's imperfect nature, his temporal organic existence, and the element of suffering are precisely the same factors used by the Infinite Mind to create within the Man a unique and robust character able to freely choose life or death."

He paused for a moment, then continued, "By attempting to leverage these factors, the Adversary unwittingly helps bring about conditions favorable for the fulfillment of the Man's intended destiny. However, the negative impact of the Adversary's oppression must at times be mitigated; otherwise the Man would be destroyed. Most humans will invariably choose life when freed of coercion; some do so despite intense pressure to do the opposite. In his weakness, the Man will be made strong."

The Watchers were confident that, despite Adam's flawed nature and the suffering inflicted upon him by the Malevolence, he would eventually consider carefully the stark reality of his temporary existence and ultimately, choose life.

The attendant responded, "Sir, the Adversary threatens his organic existence as well as his conscious spirit."

Seemingly unconcerned, the Watcher responded, "His material body is but a shell in which a seed of eternity has been planted. Though the shell will cease to exist, the seed will germinate into an unending life."

The Watchers did not speak of advantages or disadvantages regarding their purposes and mandates pertaining to man, as if they were engaged in a contest with the Dark Realm. For many ages humans believed there was a perpetual battle raging between the forces of good and the forces of evil. However, if such an ongoing battle did exist, judging from the overwhelming presence of evil throughout human history, it could have been concluded that evil always had the upper hand. But this contest, as imagined by humans, never existed.

The Dark Realm had never posed a threat to the Infinite Realm. Evil was birthed in the material universe and had been defeated from the dawn of time. Its destruction was a foregone conclusion ordained in the Infinite Realm. Every event, however unfortunate it may have been, was integrated into an intricate plan designed before the creation of time, which was the reality within which the Adversary, the Malevolence and all evil were confined.

The Mandate

For thousands of years, Mikhael watched over Adam's ancestors, including his ancient forefather Yaakov. Throughout the centuries, Mikhael guarded Yaakov's descendants and ensured their survival through persecution, wars, economic collapses, famines, and pogroms. He protected remnants of Yaakov's descendants after they had been exiled from their ancient homeland in the Near East and settled in lands throughout Europe, Africa and Asia. He watched over many who were later cast out of the Kingdom of Spain and other European lands and carried in ships to a new land.

* * * * * * *

In the Infinite Realm, a mandate was uttered, "Mikhael, go swiftly into the space-time continuum and stay alongside the Man. He is a bridge for the fourth generation. You will be his Guardian and protect him throughout his entire organic life. The Adversary will not destroy him. You will prevail and the Man will be brought safely to Olam Habah."

With singular focus, Mikhael departed instantly.

* * * * * * *

Mikhael soared through the blackness of space, like a laser beam, straight to a galaxy in the center of the observable universe. He entered the third planet from its sun, the spectacularly beautiful blue planet called Earth, where lived the conscious organic being he had been charged to protect, the man known as Adam.

Chapter 3

The Man Known as Adam

The man had been named Adan de Las Aguas by his parents, but he was called Adam by all who knew him on Earth.

However, human names are not used in the Realm. Every human being is identified by a comprehensively detailed description that precisely defines them as a unique being. The description is not spoken; it is understood. It includes the person's genetic signature, the geographic coordinates for every place they will ever be in, their history from the inception of their organic existence, their family tree, and their intended destiny. In the Infinite Realm, this naming process regularly occurs within a fraction of the smallest unit of Earth-time.

Such naming was inconceivable to humans, many of whom shared identical names and even similar appearances. At times, some even suffered harm because of mistaken or "stolen" identity. The naming process itself would have been impossible for humans, since such a detailed description of even one person would require many Earth-years to complete. Even if time were not a factor, the humans' primitive language was profoundly inadequate to formulate such a description. Even in its most advanced form, human language seemed to the Watchers as grunts and simple hand gestures did to humans. Yet the Watchers fully understood every intention conveyed by humans.

When referring to Adam, the Adversary also used a description similar to the Watchers', but with a disdainful connotation, which in human language would translate roughly as "the little human" or "the pathetic organic creature." Envious of what he suspected was a special destiny designed for the organic creatures he so thoroughly loathed and considered inferior to himself, the Adversary always minimized their worth in his communications.

Adam was a quiet, pensive person. He was creative, shy, and unassuming. He was also compassionate. Having known the pain of rejection and abuse, he could never intentionally harm or cause suffering to another person or even an animal. Cruelty and injustice were among the things he understood least and hated most. Adam often wondered why there was so much evil in his world, and why the history of his planet was marked by acts of violence perpetrated by humans against their own kind. Indeed, the threads bridging all human history were violently cruel oppression and nearly perpetual war punctuated by brief periods of peace.

Throughout the Dark Time, many humans wondered if evil had been seeded at the creation of their planet, and if so, why. It was an enigma to them. They wondered why an infinite intelligence, if such an entity even existed, would design a reality in which horrible evil could spawn and become nearly ubiquitous. Humans found this predicament so abhorrent and inconceivable that many chose to deny the existence of such an entity, rather than grapple with what was to them a profoundly irreconcilable philosophical dilemma.

They did not comprehend that freedom, which they claimed to value greatly, is esteemed highly by the Infinite Realm, despite having to deal with a temporal reality in which, at times, horrendous evil thrived. The Adversary never understood freedom, especially in the context of the Realm's penchant for ordained destinies. He believed freedom of choice was incompatible with a designed destiny. In his mind, each negated the other. He reasoned, "Destiny cannot not truly be chosen. It must be imposed or, at least, coerced."

He thought that if enough inducement or coercion was exerted, conveniently combined with opportunity, humans would inevitably choose the same dark path he had chosen. The Adversary was convinced Adam would ultimately choose that same path.

The Adversary was aware that a unique destiny had been designed for the man called Adam, but did not know its precise nature, nor did he realize the resoluteness of the Infinite Mind's purpose regarding Adam's ability to choose it. The Adversary's arrogance blinded him to this and many other realities, so he set his mind on subverting any intervention by the Realm that may have been conducive towards a special mission or destiny for Adam. He would attempt to force the Realm to abort its plans.

However, despite the Adversary's convictions, Adam was to be afforded an opportunity to freely choose his own path. To this end were committed all the powers of the Infinite Realm.

Chapter 4

The Infinite Realm

Somewhere outside time and space, beyond the material universe and the Great Beyond, lies the Infinite Realm, another dimension of reality. Though undetected by humans, this dimension is the ultimate reality from which all other realities proceed, some as mere prototypes of various aspects of the Realm. In this dimension, there are worlds upon worlds of incredible marvels.

During their organic sojourns, few humans had been allowed a glimpse of the Infinite Realm and they were completely amazed by what they saw. Many believed they had merely experienced a vivid dream or hallucination, not a reality. But no figment of the human imagination could ever come close to the mysteries of this dimension.

Humans could not imagine the size and splendor of the Realm. To them, such a place would not seem "real" and could not possibly have been real, that is, not as they defined reality. However, for those few who experienced even a taste of the Realm, nothing ever seemed more real. Henceforth, they saw nothing in their material world as permanent realities, but only as a series of temporary illusions - brief scenes of an exciting performance in a cosmic theatre that seemed alive and vibrant when viewed, but would soon pass to make room for another presentation.

In the center of the Realm stands a towering mountain, lighting up the entire kingdom with its brilliance. The height of the mountain is incalculable by any system of measure ever devised by humans, with foothills taller than the highest peaks on Earth.

At the very top of the mountain is an immense city, the seat of the Realm. The city has pearlescent walls and is perpetually illuminated. From a distance, it appears as a massive galaxy glowing with lights of different colors, reminiscent of the aurora borealis at which humans marveled for many ages.

The Majestic Throne, which rules over all realities, is in the midst of the city at the mountain's top. The throne, which is formed out of a massive, gleaming sapphire stone, is surrounded by a body of water with the most curious qualities. The water is calm and peaceful, yet in almost constant flux. It simultaneously has the appearance of flowing water, solid ice, and molten glass. More than one hundred million attendants serve the throne.

Along the edges of the Realm, the only regions not perpetually illuminated, are falls from which iridescent waters cascade audaciously from high mountains and crash into bottomless glowing lakes. The singular source of these waters is an enormous river that proceeds from the sea surrounding the Majestic Throne and flows down the great mountain to the lesser mountains.

The Realm is not bound by time and space, nor subject to the force of gravity. Some beings in the Realm seem to always stand at an angle. Others initially appear as a brilliant horizontal line of what seems to be electricity, but then instantly morph into a living being, standing upright, in bodily form. Some seem to exist in perpetual orbit. Many beings appear to be flying, although few of them actually have wings. Among those few, are the exalted beings who serve as entourage of the Majestic Throne.

An ancient human seer recorded an uncanny encounter with these astonishing beings. He described a stormy wind coming out of the north and a great cloud engulfed in flames with brightness around it. In the midst of the fire was the color of burning coals, and out of it came the likeness of four living creatures who sparkled like burnished brass. Each creature had the appearance of a man but with four faces and four wings. Each had the face of a man on what seemed to be the front of its body, the face of a lion on the right, an ox on the left, and an eagle behind. They each had what seemed to be human hands under each of its four wings. Two of the wings were extended upward and appeared joined to the wings of the other beings in the entourage. Their other two wings covered their bodies. These beings always faced the direction in which they chose to go, never turning right or left. They glowed like coals of fire, like blazing torches. Without ever turning, they moved as quickly as the flashes of lightning that went out from the fire and the surrounding brightness.

Each of the creatures had what appeared to be hooved feet. Near the feet of each creature hovered a strange emerald-colored wheel. It was actually an immense wheel within another wheel. The ancient seer wrote that the rings of these wheels were so high they were dreadful, and full of eyes all around. When the creatures moved, the wheels went with them. As the wheels spun, they created an incredibly loud humming sound. However, what is even stranger is that the life essence of the creatures; what humans called the spirit, was actually in the wheels as well.

Over the heads of the living creatures was the appearance of a platform of sky, but emerald in color, rather than blue. Under the platform, the tips of each of the creatures' wings met as if fused together. When they moved, the sound of their wings was like the noise of a great waterfall.

Above the emerald platform was a throne with the appearance of an incredibly massive sapphire stone. The being upon the throne had the form of a human engulfed in flames from his loins downward. He was surrounded by a bright glow, similar in appearance to a rainbow.

The creatures described by the seer were but a few of the many Luminous Beings of the Infinite Realm, all of whom move so rapidly in space-time that, when they allowed themselves to be seen by humans, they appeared as flashes of lightning. Rarely were they ever even detected by human eyes. But, on certain occasions, for specific purposes, they moved slowly enough to be clearly seen and heard by humans.

All Luminous Beings emanate light—some a dazzling white light, others a bluish glow, and some have the appearance of burning embers radiating intense heat. Most of the humans who had seen these burning beings, fearing they would not survive very long in proximity to them, collapsed into unconsciousness. Another ancient seer remained sick and confined to his bed for three weeks after only one encounter with one of these glowing beings.

The Luminous Beings have always communicated by transmitting thoughts, intentions, and feelings directly to the minds of other beings. Although they were able to convey messages with spoken or written human language, they had no need for this crude form of communication as humans once did. During their organic experience, some humans were caused to understand messages transmitted by beings from the Infinite Realm as if these had been expressed in human language. However, in reality they had merely been enabled to understand the essence of the intent of the messages conveyed.

The Great Hall

The Great Hall is an immense and elegant structure, near the city at the top of the high peak in the center of the Infinite Realm. The Great Hall is within the Realm and yet appears to be suspended in the space of the material universe, as if it were floating in a portable container of space. One of its functions was to serve as a venue where the being who had once been an exalted prince of the Realm, but later was exiled to the material universe, could appear in his official capacity.

The walls, ceiling, and floor of the Great Hall are crystal clear. When looking out from within the Hall, one seems to be floating in the darkness of space. It is a place of mystifying beauty. All around, above, below, and even through this intriguing place, all the wonders of the universe—galaxies, constellations, stars, and planets—are visible, as if one is soaring through space in a massive and completely transparent spacecraft.

There is no perceivable limit to the height of the walls of the Hall, nor to its width or depth. Its dimensions vary, relative to the nature of the proceedings taking place within it. The Great Hall can be as enormous as the boundless heavens observable by mankind or as small and intimate as a child's bedroom. Similar to many great structures in the Realm, the Great Hall has gleaming white, iridescent pillars soaring upward and is illuminated by the radiance of glowing Luminous Beings that, from a distance, appear as bright stars.

The proceedings in the Great Hall are orderly and conducted according to strict protocol, with exact precision and majestic dignity.

On one occasion, the Council of Watchers, a tribunal of twenty-four mysterious Luminous Beings, had assembled in the Hall.

On that special convening, the Council and the Infinite Mind discussed the life and destiny of a certain conscious organic being, a human. From beyond a portal unseen by humans, a gate between the temporal universe and the Infinite Realm, Watchers were assembled in council and observed the man known as Adam.

The Council referred to Adam as a child/man/being, as if all stages of his life were happening concurrently. They spoke, as if he was, simultaneously, yet to be born, but, currently living, and as if he had already died, but was still alive in another, non-organic, form. In the Infinite Realm, past, present, and future tenses of language, as used in the human realm, are irrelevant, because time is not a relevant measure in this dimension. But, at a certain interval in Earth-time, Adam, the child/man, was languishing and would continue to agonize in nearly perpetual suffering until events were altered.

Since the Infinite Realm exists outside the boundaries of time, communications about events in Earth-time transcend the moment in which these events took, are taking, or will take place. However, in the dimension of time, Adam was now targeted for imminent destruction by the Adversary. This phenomenon was a great mystery designed by the time master.

Chapter 5

The Time Master

Time, as known by temporal organic beings, has never existed in the Infinite Realm, though it once ruled over the material universe with unyielding severity. Although time was a reality affecting other dimensions, events in the Realm were never measured by or subject to it as in the space-time continuum, within which were contained unfavorable events and consequences not intended for infinite permanence.

For humans, time was a severe master. But it was no more than an illusion, albeit a harsh one, a relative measure of the occurrence of events rather than an objective reality. Every present moment became enshrined in their memory the instant humans experienced it.

The present, the only reality in which they existed, was constantly flowing into and becoming that which they called the past, never to be repeated again despite how hard they tried to hold on to or recreate it. Within the bounds of time, as experienced by humans, every moment became the past before they could even describe it. Therefore, most humans disdained the present moment, their only true reality, in favor of an ever-elusive experience they could never relive or a future of which they had no assurance.

The Infinite Mind, who is the Time Master, designed and brought into being the observable universe, the Great Beyond, and all other realities; including realms and life forms that were visible and invisible to human beings. Some realities remained completely sealed in mystery and undetectable even by the most advanced technology ever devised by humans throughout their organic existence.

One mystery was how the Infinite Mind caused the universe to exist as a cohesive unit, holding galaxies and celestial bodies in their precise circuits, maintaining the complex interdependency of all earthly organic life forms and the forces of nature in a delicate balance. All life forms in all dimensions proceeded from, exist within, and are sustained by the Infinite Mind. Yet, for the most part, the Infinite Mind was unknown to humans.

The Infinite Mind transcends time and sees the past, present, and future concurrently, as mere facets of a single event unfolding in space-time. Seeing the end from the beginning, he is able to bring about a desired result when necessary. Therefore, when referring to a determined destiny, the Infinite Mind speaks as if all has already occurred, like a tale that has already been told. The phases of Adam's life were but scenes in a drama foreseen in the Infinite Realm ages before his organic birth.

This phenomenon, which is as natural in this mysterious realm as it was supernatural in the human world, was unfathomable to humans and a source of great frustration to the renegade prince who came to be known as the Adversary.

Chapter 6

The Adversary

On one occasion, a dark presence appeared in and diminished the radiance of the usually brilliant Great Hall. It was the ancient Adversary of the Realm, seeking an audience before the Great Council.

The Adversary, a perverse dignitary and rogue prince, was formerly an exalted member of the esteemed Council of Luminous Beings held in the highest regard. But he allowed his heart to be poisoned by arrogance, envy, and a sense of entitlement that made him profoundly bitter and resentful. Though once known as the Shining One, he came to abhor light. He now cringes and cannot see clearly in light, feeling his way around like a blind creature.

In the Infinite Realm, the Adversary could appear only as his true self. But when he appeared in the human realm, he always disguised himself, concealing his true nature. When the Adversary made himself visible to human eyes, something he rarely did, he always took on a deceptively attractive or seductive form, at times clothed in flamboyantly dazzling light. After the veil was removed from their eyes, some humans were able to perceive his true self. He preyed on these particular humans with exceptionally cruel determination. Most humans, however, remained unaware of his existence.

The Adversary would cover himself with a thick dark fog. Were he visible to human eyes in his true form, he would appear as a decaying creature. As a decomposing organic body exuding a foul stench, he reeked of hatred, envy, bitter rage, obsessive arrogance, and smoldering resentment over perceived slights to what he believed was his exalted person. When he entered a confined space on Earth in bodily form, the air temperature often became unusually cold.

His form was grotesquely deformed as a result of fierce battles during his failed coup attempt against the Majestic Throne. His narrow, pale eyes appeared hollow and were housed in a completely transparent frame that he covered with a long, dark, hooded cloak. His voice was generally an echoing, cacophonous growl, but at times of great stress, rage, or fear, he would let out a raspy shriek or an eerie howl.

However, the Adversary had once been a spectacular being of exquisite beauty and regal majesty. He held the highest rank of the Infinite Guard and, as a highly-esteemed Counselor, stood alongside the very Majestic Throne in the midst of the remarkable fiery stones. Harmonious music emanated from his very being, as fragrant essence would proceed from exotic flowers or the sound of wind chimes when caressed by a gentle breeze.

Unfortunately, the Adversary became filled with pride and an exaggerated sense of self-worth. A seed of bitterness and resentment grew within him, due to an irreconcilable disappointment, which was that he could never be equal to the highest of all living conscious beings, the sovereign who sits on the Majestic Throne ruling over all realities.

Rancor seethed within him and festered until his outward appearance changed to reflect his inner self, which had become hideous. Of his former qualities, he retained only his extraordinary intelligence and power. Bitterness caused what was once great wisdom to be reduced to mere intellect, which he further perverted by using it only for cunning deception, manipulation, and destruction.

The Infinite Mind appealed to this being, as a father would entreat a beloved son, before he had traveled far on his new dark path.

"You have chosen a path that will become increasingly darker as you travel on it. Eventually, all light will be extinguished from it. Will you not turn from this path before you are no longer able to see your way back? There are other paths available for your choosing."

But the Adversary rejected all entreaties and became an avowed enemy of the Realm as well as every being in allegiance or associated with the Infinite Mind. His very name was changed to reflect what he had become in the essence of his being—the Adversary.

Thus, began the Dark Time.

Chapter 7

The Dark Time

Seething in discontent, the Adversary began planning a rebellion. Apparently convinced he was undetected, he would enter the nether regions of the material universe through portals used by only a few of the Guard of the Realm, to develop his mutinous plans to overthrow the Lord of All Realities. Under a self-induced delusion, or perhaps genuinely ignorant of the fact that the Infinite Mind sees all corners of all realities, the Adversary conspired to garner support among the Guard of the Realm. He persuaded a third of them to join him in an attack against the Majestic Throne. The rest remained resolute in their loyalty to the Throne.

The Adversary attempted to mount his revolt in the Infinite Realm, but was immediately repelled and forcefully ejected from the Realm along with his fellow conspirators.

War broke out in the heavens and spread throughout the material universe. Mikhael, a mighty warrior, and his armies fought against the Adversary and his horde. More than one hundred million nonmortal beings waged fierce battles over the course of many Earth-ages in the greatest war ever fought. It caused inconceivable destruction. Much of the observable universe suffered immense devastation. Entire galaxies were laid waste, their lights nearly extinguished.

The Adversary's attempted coup resulted in utter failure, but had it not been for the protection of the Watchers and the Infinite Mind, most of the universe would have been utterly destroyed. Needless to say, the Adversary was removed from his exalted position in the Council. He and his cohorts were expelled from the Infinite Realm, exiled deep within a galaxy near the center of the observable universe and confined to a planet known as Earth.

The energy of the force with which the Adversary was cast out of the Realm resembled a powerful bolt of lightning striking the Earth, causing massive destruction. Humans wondered what caused such devastating effects, some of which remained for thousands of years.

For many ages, the rebels wandered aimlessly throughout the planet and its atmosphere, creating chaos and mayhem at every opportunity.

The Adversary developed a special hatred for the organic beings known as humans, who were conspicuously different from all other organic beings. They were not merely sentient beings; they had *real* consciousness—unique self-awareness, intelligence, and creative abilities found in no other organic life forms. In far too many ways, they resembled the Infinite Mind. Man was, indeed, the pinnacle of all organic beings.

The Adversary profoundly resented being exiled and imprisoned on a planet with humans. He had a foreboding suspicion about them, rooted in his fear that the conscious organic creatures he so thoroughly detested would be elevated above him. His fear added fuel to his already intense resentment. The extermination of all human life became his all-consuming purpose. He longed to destroy not only their bodies and minds, but also their spirits, the true essence of all conscious beings. If that were not possible, he would settle for destroying any aspect of their existence. When he failed to destroy them, he would torture, undermine, or enslave the humans.

The Adversary stole the unique qualities, such as free will, that distinguished humans from lower organic life forms. He stole their time, the means by which they measured the quantity of their organic existence, and robbed them of joy. He deceived them and distorted their perception of reality, causing them to see good as evil and evil as good. The Adversary perverted every aspect of the human realm.

So thoroughly did he destroy their dignity that they blindly sacrificed what they most needed; trading love, lasting relationships, contentment, and peace, for material possessions, power, and temporal pleasure.

The Adversary provoked separations within the human family. Love of family and community was often manipulated and twisted into rabid xenophobic nationalism, which eventually was used as justification for the oppression and annihilation of entire populations of humans. Even some of Earth's most gentle people would justify and lend support to violent oppression and wars of conquest, convinced these were necessary for their security or the protection of their interests. Through their many wars, humans nearly destroyed themselves and their entire planet.

As a result of rampant violence and oppression, like undulating waves, swelling masses of oppressed people roamed the Earth, seeking refuge from cruel persecution. Some were welcomed and granted asylum by certain nations. Others were refused shelter, which resulted in many generations of humans becoming perpetual exiles.

The Adversary and his Malevolence caused humans to become intoxicated with a feeling of self-importance, a reflection of their unseen master's arrogance. Due to their ever-growing knowledge and technological advancements, every generation thought themselves superior to their predecessors. The Adversary caused mankind to see humility, a quality he never understood, as contemptible weakness. Raw, arrogant power was seen as a virtue. The Malevolence promoted fear, hostility, and perpetual distrust among humans. Eventually, humans came to live in, and accepted as normal, a state of perpetual violence.

Eventually, the Malevolence wove itself into the fabric of all aspects of human society. Man's eyes became thoroughly blinded, as if covered by a heavy veil. People advocated, even protested, for things that threatened their existence as a species.

Humans had been endowed with an extraordinary creative capacity, which could have been used for either good or evil. Unfortunately, under the influence and at times the direct control of the Malevolence, most of man's innovations, though originally intended for good, resulted in great evil. Ingenious at inventing and refining tools of destruction, man consistently created more advanced forms of killing, including what some called sanitized warfare. Using their advanced technology, including remotely controlled missiles, drones, and robotic soldiers, humans were able to destroy individuals, cities, and entire countries with mere keystrokes—and not be affected emotionally by the resulting carnage.

Responsibility for the killing and maiming of their fellow humans, including many innocents not engaged in warfare, was officially shared by many, but accepted by none. This new type of killing did not seem real to humans, as war had become much like a game of fantasy. Euphemistic terms, such as "collateral damage" and "friendly fire," were used to disguise the grotesque brutality of warfare. Humans became so depraved that, eventually, slaughter of innocents, random mass murders, and horrific acts of terror were seen as commonplace; even normal. Indeed, these events became so prevalent that they altered the face of human societies throughout their world.

Despite many desperate attempts to do so, humans were never able to find their way to lasting peace. They groped for peace like blind men stumbling in deep darkness, looking for a door they could never find. Even in the absence of war, they had no peace. Humans had been duped into trading peace for inferior commodities.

Ultimately, the Adversary took from them everything of any lasting value, leaving them with no hope—except the one hope of which most humans were unaware.

Bent on destroying Adam and sabotaging his destiny, the Adversary began oppressing him well before he reached the age of reason. Though unaware of the specifics of the unique destiny that had been planned for Adam before his birth, the Adversary knew the Infinite Realm had a special focus on Adam's ancestors. Consequently, he relentlessly persecuted them with sadistic fury, nearly destroying three generations of Adam's ancestors and effectively jeopardizing Adam's organic birth.

The Adversary lurked in the shadows of Adam's family history, performing his nefarious acts in the darkness of unawareness and denial. He was in the center of every horrific event and behind every tragedy, causing the untimely deaths of some of their little ones, orchestrating freak accidents, and destroying others in war.

He promoted lifestyles that resulted in chronic physical disease, mental illness, poverty, and shame. He burdened them with addictions to alcohol, drugs, sex, rage, and superstition.

But from the moment the decree was issued in the Infinite Realm, the Watchers were committed to shielding and guiding the man called Adam, who was to be the bridge of the fourth generation. The Watchers were charged with providing Adam the opportunity to freely choose or reject his destiny and to sustain him with hope throughout this process. Hope was always present in Adam's life, though it was also long deferred. It was his beacon. He held on to it tenaciously, but at times it seemed to Adam that his hope was no more than a wishful longing, an elusive dream of a better future that he could barely imagine. Shelomoh, an ancient Eastern monarch, once wrote, "Hope deferred makes the heart sick."

The deferral of Adam's hope did make his heart sick, but without hope, he would have completely surrendered to the evil that stalked him, so thoroughly had his spirit been crushed.

Through many long and lonely nights of excruciating mental anguish, as a child and later as a grown man, Adam poured out his most intimate and profound pain to the deity of whom he had often heard his parents speak. He doubted the deity heard his pleas or cared about his pain, but not knowing what else to do, he continued pleading. Adam spent many nights perplexed, wondering about the reasons for his affliction. Was the deity punishing him? Was there any purpose to his life and for his suffering, or was he merely an insignificant and worthless mass of conscious, organic matter groping in darkness, banging against walls of circumstances outside his control? Eventually, Adam began to wonder if the deity even existed. He began wondering, "What if there is no God."

Adam's eyes were covered by a dark veil that prevented him from seeing even the possibility that his life had any purpose at all, much less a special destiny. But throughout his life, there was evidence of the seeds of destiny.

Chapter 8

Seeds of Destiny

Adam's family lived in a small shack that could hardly be called a house, near a rugged bluff with a majestic view of the restless Caribbean Sea. His rustic hometown was nestled on the coast of a beautiful but impoverished island, an idyllic tropical paradise. The island's history hearkened back to the Old World in the continent known as Europe. Although their language and most of their customs originated in Spain, they also had vestiges of indigenous and African cultures.

Adam's family was fairly large. He had four brothers and four sisters, although the organic eyes of an additional younger brother were closed in death soon after birth. Only after reaching adulthood did Adam learn about his deceased younger brother, who was never given a name—that is, not by humans.

When Adam was still an infant, his father went in search of work opportunities in another land. He temporarily left Adam's mother in dire poverty while tending to six young children. One hot afternoon, when Adam was less than one Earth-year in age, his mother placed him in a hammock to enjoy the tropical ocean breeze as he slept. The hammock was behind their small house, just outside the kitchen. It was suspended between two trees, in an area with a concrete floor. After making sure the child was comfortable, Adam's mother went into the kitchen and sat at the table with a neighbor to enjoy some conversation over a cup of coffee, a welcomed distraction from her arduous chores.

Shortly after sitting down, the women heard a disturbing sound—an unusually loud rush of wind, followed by a thump and an unsettling sharp cry. Adam's mother immediately looked out the window to check on her child, for the sound was not a cry of hunger or discomfort. It was a shriek of fear or pain.

Apparently, a violent gust of wind had shaken and flipped the hammock. Adam had fallen from a height of about four feet, his head smashing against the concrete floor. His mother's heart raced as she and her neighbor ran to pick up her child. What followed next was even more disconcerting than his fall. Almost as soon as it started, Adam's crying stopped abruptly.

The young mother quickly lifted the baby off the floor and ran into the house. Adam's small body stiffened and convulsed, his head jerked backward, and his pupils rolled up. Barely breathing, he appeared dead to his mother, who was aghast and did not know what to do. Never had she been faced with such an urgent crisis. She berated herself for having left her child unattended.

At the time, the family's town was small, remote and undeveloped and had no emergency response system. Adam's family did not own a vehicle; in fact, Adam's mother never learned to drive. After laying her child on a bed and covering him with a blanket, she immediately sent her oldest son in search of the local doctor.

She knew it could take quite some time for her eldest son to reach the doctor's office and for them to return home. Meanwhile, her child's life seemed to be hanging in the balance. Not knowing what else to do, the mother and her neighbor did the only thing they believed they could do to immediately help the child. As most of the island people did in critical times of trouble, they prayed to their deity. Feeling as if that which she feared most had come upon her, Adam's mother and her neighbor placed their hands on the child and pleaded for his life. Then they watched anxiously for a sign of improvement as they waited for the doctor to arrive.

An hour later, there was still no improvement and no doctor. Adam's mother feared that her son would soon fall into his final sleep. She looked at his small body—barely breathing, still and stiff as a corpse. Though her neighbor remained confident that the child would recover fully, Adam's mother nearly gave up hope and tried to prepare her heart for what she thought was the inevitable death of her infant son. She wondered whom he would have become and what he would have accomplished had she not been so careless. Berating herself again, she wondered how she could possibly break such horrible news to her husband, of whom she had developed a profound fear.

Although she struggled to face the inevitability of losing her little child, Adam's mother was unable to do so. She could not accept such a horrible loss. Her heart broken, she sobbed bitterly.

* * * * * * *

In the Infinite Realm, the Watchers observed. They had already determined to intervene and nullify the intent of the Malevolence.

* * * * * * *

Adam's mother thought she saw a change in her son's condition, but she was afraid to hope. Looking again, she realized she did see a change. The child's small body seemed to have relaxed somewhat. Within a few minutes, he seemed to be breathing normally and sleeping restfully, as if nothing at all had happened. Suddenly, the child's eyes fluttered and opened, as if awakening from a peaceful sleep. He uttered a slight cry, not the shriek of pain and shock the women had previously heard, but a healthy baby's normal cry for nourishment or comfort.

Adam's mother was amazed and speechless. Her child had somehow miraculously recovered. An incomprehensible miracle had occurred and she was immeasurably thankful, but she also felt strangely afraid.

Adam's mother cherished this memory and spoke often of it to Adam and her other children. Perhaps it was her way of assuring her son in later years that he was special. The story had little effect on Adam, or so he thought. He heard his mother tell the story often throughout his childhood, but he thought it nothing more than a delusion shared by two superstitious women. He wasn't convinced that anything supernatural had occurred. Nevertheless, he was intrigued by one conspicuous detail. Adam's mother would always end the story by recounting how her neighbor assured her, with uncanny confidence, that he would recover fully. The woman expressed an unusually strong conviction that Adam had been chosen for a special destiny.

According to Adam's mother, her neighbor claimed to have seen a ring of fire around his bed as they prayed. When her neighbor saw this phenomenon, the woman gasped, wondering how fire could have suddenly flared up. She feared that they now had another, even worse, emergency to deal with.

The neighbor uttered in dismay, "Ay, Dios mio, como puede ser?" ["Oh, my God, how can this be?"] Then, in an instant, the fire vanished. At first, she was perplexed, but then realized she had been granted a glance into an unseen reality. She believed her vision meant that a special destiny was prepared for the child; that he was supernaturally protected and would recover fully. Adam's mother did not witness this amazing sight, but she was utterly convinced of the truth of her neighbor's assertion. With her own eyes, she had seen an incredible miracle in its own right—the complete recovery of her son who about an hour before had been as good as dead. She would never forget that day.

At a deep level, Adam sometimes wondered if there were, indeed, realities unseen by most humans. But, by the time he had become an adolescent, he abandoned the memory of that story. If he had really been selected for some special destiny by supernatural beings, Adam wished they had chosen someone else, since his ordeal of suffering and mental oppression began at a very young age. He wondered what destiny could possibly be worth that emotional pain. Adam felt as if a certain darkness had been born with him. His ordeal seemed like a perpetual nightmare and he longed for it to end. He could not recall the inception of what was to be a long dark night.

Chapter 9

The Long Night

The Malevolence stalked Adam until he was isolated and imprisoned by shame and fear. As a child, he experienced emotionally painful abuse and nearly perpetual fear. Adam kept this torment neatly compartmentalized in his mind and separated from the other aspects of his life he felt were normal. Later, he endured years of repeated and profound disappointment. The abuse he suffered engraved, almost indelibly, shame, self-loathing, and dysfunction into his psyche and character. Perhaps the most painful aspect of his struggle was having to bear it alone and in silence.

It all started with one traumatic event. When humans were profoundly affected by a life-changing experience, especially as children, the pivotal experience forever divided everything in their lives into before and after. The pivotal event for Adam occurred when he was a very young boy, although he never knew exactly how old he had been. It was the first link in a chain of events that would ultimately alter the course of his life. His young life was to undergo a major and permanent change. After that, Adam would never be the same.

Adam's innocent childhood came to an abrupt end on one of the most traumatic nights of his life. It was the end of carefree and imaginative playing with his plastic menagerie and his train set, the end of childish visions of a world he had thought was basically good, and the end of his hopes for a happy, normal life. That fateful evening, Adam was pulled into a world that was darker and a form of abuse that was more traumatic than he had ever known. The tool used to subvert Adam's destiny was one who had also been victimized by the Malevolence.

Adam's mother punished him that night for an infraction of which he was innocent. The young boy obediently got out of the bathtub, as ordered by his mother, and stood wet, naked, and ashamed—crying as she hit him with a leather belt. Adam did not understand what he had done wrong. But he felt he must have done something, so he did not protest or declare his innocence. That would have only invited more punishment, so he just stood there, humiliated and naked, as his mother hit him.

Despite the fear, family dysfunction, and grinding poverty he had experienced before that night, Adam's life had seemed normal to him. That night marked the end of his "normal" life and the beginning of an interminable nightmare. For several years, Adam would secretly endure a most humiliating abuse. He was so young when it began, that he didn't understand what was happening to him, yet, he knew intuitively that it was evil – horribly evil.

Over time, Adam suffered prolonged mental anguish that severely limited the choices available to him and had a profoundly negative effect on every aspect of his life. His negative responses to his distress came to define his personality, his character, and how he viewed himself and the world he lived in.

Chapter 10

Adam's World

Adam and his siblings were taken away from the Caribbean island they knew as home when he was only two years old. Out of economic necessity, Adam's mother reluctantly moved to a large city, then known as New York, where Adam's father had been working for almost two years. Most of Adam's life was spent in that city where millions of other humans made their homes.

His neighborhood had many historic buildings and attractive homes, then known as brownstones, which Adam loved and considered to be elegant structures. They were reminiscent of homes he saw in old motion picture films and vintage photographs of his city.

Adam lived in a quaint area near a famous bridge, called the Brooklyn Bridge, of which he had heard but had only seen in pictures. He was proud of his neighborhood, and he came to love the bridge as if it was his very own. But Adam had no idea how close he actually lived to the bridge because he was rarely ever allowed to leave his house except to visit family, attend school or church, or perhaps go to a store or medical appointment with one of his parents.

Home, school, and church represented the boundaries of Adam's world. Still, he felt very comfortable in his neighborhood and enjoyed what little he had been able to see of it. He especially loved his school. School was his sanctuary, a haven from the fear and abuse he secretly suffered at home.

In a sense, Adam lived in two completely different worlds with conflicting values. Humans had many worlds within worlds with layers of contradiction. The first of Adam's worlds was the one seen by his grandmother, aunts and uncles, and the people with whom his parents worshipped at church. In that world, Adam's family was led by an austere, but ostensibly upstanding and devout man. That world displayed a facade of regular church attendance, worship music, and strict religious observance.

It was a world of many rules and many prohibitions. When Adam was a child, his family never attended a movie or went to a beach. The wearing of pants and cosmetics was forbidden for girls and women. Card playing, popular music, and dancing were all considered evil, and alcohol was strictly prohibited. Only once did Adam's father take his children to visit a popular amusement park. Perhaps this concession was made after Adam's maternal grandmother and other relatives admonished his father about his family's need for occasional recreational activities.

Adam's other world was one his relatives and the people with whom his parents worshipped never got to see. It was a world of dark secrets, in which he and his siblings cowered in fear and where some suffered humiliating abuse. This other world was permeated with an overwhelming terror of the volatile anger and unpredictable violent outbursts of Adam's overbearing biological father.

Adam lived in utter terror of the man he and his siblings called Papi, a strangely contradictory term of endearment meaning "Daddy." In Adam's family, fear was cloaked as respect and beatings masqueraded as parental discipline. Adam witnessed his father savagely beating his sisters and brothers, in sudden fits of rage, for almost any infraction or irritation. On two different occasions, his father broke an umbrella over the backs of two of Adam's brothers. Curiously, Adam's two youngest sisters were completely spared from the violent abuse of their father, who was already aging when they were born, and died when they were still very young.

Adam's fearful, compliant nature spared him from his father's physical violence. Aside from being slapped or swatted with a belt a few times by his mother, he was rarely ever hit. Adam's mother was generally very gentle and affectionate with him. His father was neither gentle or affectionate. He once struck Adam over the head with Adam's sneaker. He didn't like the way Adam was carrying them; one over his chest and the other over his shoulder, as the other boys in his school did. Though Adam rarely suffered physical violence, as did most of his siblings, the humiliation he endured; a violence of a different nature, profoundly harmed and nearly destroyed the essence of his person, that is, his spirit.

One day, when Adam was only about six Earth-years in age, his father walked into their apartment in a cheerful mood, carrying bags of groceries. He placed the bags on the dining room table, sat down, and took a pack of chewing gum out of one of the bags. Suddenly, one of Adam's sisters, who was about eight years of age, in a moment of childish impishness, grabbed the pack of chewing gum and ran down the hall laughing.

A man with a sound mind might have been somewhat irritated and scolded the child, or perhaps even laughed at her childishness. Unfortunately, Adam's father's mind was anything but sound. He exploded in a searing rage, grabbed the nearest object, and hurled it at his little daughter.

The nearest object was a hammer.

Adam watched the hammer fly, as if in slow motion, down the hallway and straight at his sister. In his child's mind, Adam was convinced the hammer would not—could not—hit his sister. That was unthinkable. Like a shroud, covering their faces, stealing their very breath, and rendering them mute, terror descended over Adam and his siblings. Adam wished he could stop the hammer in midflight, but it flew as a guided missile directly toward his sister. Adam felt some relief when he saw the hammer hit the wall. But, his relief was short lived because the hammer bounced off the wall and struck his sister on the back. The little girl collapsed. She suffered a terrible punishment that day for behaving as the child she was. Being unable to do anything about what he had seen caused Adam great emotional distress.

Adam was in shock. Never had he seen anyone, in anger, throw something as dangerous as a hammer at anyone else. The idea of his father angrily throwing a hammer at his own young daughter, especially for so minor an infraction as grabbing a pack of chewing gum, was unbearable.

That horrible sight filled Adam with overwhelming terror and confusion. Adam's heart collapsed, just as his sister did when struck by the hammer. How could his father have done such a thing? Though he was afraid to allow himself to experience anger, Adam was angry— furiously angry—at such a horrible injustice. But he could do nothing about it. He was only a small child and dared not express his indignation. Held in the firm grip of an overwhelming fear, none of the children, including Adam, dared to even venture to help their sister. The scene was so terrifying that Adam found himself frozen by fear, a fear he remained captive to until, finally, his father died when Adam was about sixteen years old.

When Adam was twelve years old, his father decided to move the family. Adam was devastated. He was taken from the neighborhood he grew up in and came to love; the clock tower he saw every day on his way to and from school, the impressive cathedrals, and the stately court buildings. As if he were losing a dear friend, Adam grieved the loss of the picturesque brownstones - especially his favorite; a redbrick house situated a few blocks from his apartment that was completely covered on one side by bright green ivy. The red house reminded Adam of stories he enjoyed reading by one of his favorite authors, a man named O'Henry, who wrote about New York during a bygone era.

Adam had many good memories of his former home and neighborhood. He remembered pleasant holiday gatherings with his family; especially his grandmother, uncles, aunts, and cousins on his mother's side. He recalled smelling the sweet fragrance of honeysuckle as he walked home from church with his mother. He also had fond memories of his elementary school, despite some traumatic experiences during his first year there.

One of Adam's earliest memories was of an incident that occurred his very first week of school. He was physically attacked by an older boy. One of his older sisters, the same girl at whom his father had thrown a hammer, defended him. On another occasion, Adam's first-grade teacher, an older woman who had apparently grown frustrated with her profession, became very impatient with her students. Adam and the other children in his class felt intimidated by her size and demeanor. She was a large woman who always seemed angry and would often yell at the children. One day she became extremely irritated. Feeling that the children were too physically close to her, she abruptly kicked Adam's desk into his chest while he was sitting at it.

But, despite these negative experiences, school was Adam's haven, his only sanctuary. He thought of school as his little hut—though, of course, he never said that to anyone but himself. School was the one place where he felt relatively safe. It was where he was seen, heard, and liked by others, as well as recognized for his academic and artistic abilities.

Adam's family's first move, which occurred when he was just an infant, was from their small rustic Caribbean island to the sprawling city of New York. But the first move Adam could remember, which was also the one that impacted him most, happened when he was an adolescent. This move not only plucked him from his school, the only place he truly loved and felt safe in, it also took him away from the few acquaintances he had made. He found himself a pariah, an unwelcomed outsider in a hostile school environment and a violent neighborhood. From that time forward, throughout his formative years, Adam would always be an outsider in every neighborhood his family moved to.

The area Adam's father moved the family to, no doubt thinking he was improving their quality of life, was then known as Williamsburg. Unfortunately, at the time, it was infested with gang violence and illegal drug activity. From the very first day at school, Adam was viciously harassed in this neighborhood.

Adam was different from most other teenage boys—more pensive and creative, less talented in sports. Because of this, many of his peers rejected him and treated him with contempt.

One day, Adam was pushed past his limit. The leader of the pack of boys who regularly harassed Adam with taunts and humiliating insults, started hitting him in front of the entire class. Adam had had enough. Though he was not a fighter, he fought back as hard as he could, but his defensive blows had no impact on the boy attacking him. The teacher sided with Adam and sent the other boy out of the classroom. This infuriated the boy, who now set his mind on making Adam pay for his being embarrassed in front of the class.

After school, the boy and his buddies chased Adam down the block and around the corner, all the while hurling snowballs and insults at him. It was a dismally cold, snowy day. The pavement was wet and slippery. Some of the snowballs were packed tight, but none of them actually hit Adam hard enough to hurt him, that is, not physically.

The teenage boys, just like the men in this neighborhood, were accustomed to violence. Adam knew they were capable of physically battering a person without any hesitation. He had seen the dean of his school walking with crutches and had been told that the man's leg had been broken by some of the older boys in the school. But Adam's greatest concern was the humiliation to which he was being subjected, in front of all the students and adults passing by.

Adam knew he could not fight off a pack of teenaged boys with his bare hands. All he could do was run. He ran as fast as he could, but the snow and ice on the pavement slowed him down. Still, Adam continued running. He ran for many years. He ran from harassment, from humiliation, and from shame resulting from the abuse he secretly endured.

Several people passed by and saw what was taking place, but none stopped to help. But then, Adam slipped and almost fell in front of a small, elderly woman who was walking toward him and the other boys. Trying to prevent Adam from falling, the elderly woman grabbed his arm to steady him. She attempted to scare away his pursuers by shaking her umbrella and yelling at them in Spanish. But it was to no avail. She was old and feeble, and could not intimidate them. They laughed her to scorn. Adam was horribly ashamed. He thought it should have been him defending an old woman, rather than the other way around.

The encounter with the elderly woman allowed Adam to place some distance between himself and the boys, who kept coming after him like a pack of ravenous wolves. He slipped again, this time falling face down on the cold, wet pavement. Adam had been so focused on trying to get away that he hadn't noticed a man with a large umbrella and a gray fedora hat walking toward them.

Adam fell at the man's feet. Immediately, he felt someone grabbing him by his arm and pulling him to his feet. At first, he saw only the man's black shoes and the bottom of his cuffed pants. When he was pulled to his feet by the man and was able to see his face clearly, Adam was shocked and horribly ashamed. It was his father.

Adam's father was an imposing figure, not a man to be trifled with. The boys retreated as soon as they realized the man intended to stop their abuse of Adam. Before they retreated, the leader of the pack, the boy who had attacked Adam in school, yelled out an insult meant as a justification for their abuse. When Adam and his father arrived home, Adam went to his room to change out of his wet clothes. His father went into the kitchen. From his room, Adam overheard his father whispering to his mother, in a hushed tone, about the incident after school. His father whispered the insult the leader of the gang of boys had yelled out about Adam, the very insult Adam believed was meant as justification for the abuse they had inflicted on him.

Adam detected disappointment in his father's tone. No, it was more than disappointment, Adam felt that his father was ashamed of him. This made Adam feel even more ashamed of himself. Listening to his father whispering to his mother about him, Adam felt a profound pain that lasted many years.

He would have preferred to be beaten to a bloody pulp by the gang of boys who had chased him after school, rather than experience such emotional pain. The Malevolence was thoroughly pleased. Undetected by Adam or anyone in his family, the Malevolence lurked in the shadows of his home that day. With great satisfaction, they permeated the air with venomous emotions.

This was not the first time that Adam overheard his father speak disapprovingly of him. Adam did not know why his father was displeased with him. Adam was always obedient to his parents, and would never dare cause any trouble. He always did well in school, consistently earning high grades, and receiving awards for academic achievement. But he knew that his awards would never make him acceptable to his father or even to himself. He felt hopelessly inadequate and disheartened. Adam never felt loved by his father, nor did he ever experience any show of affection from him. On the contrary, he felt terror, resentment, and sometimes even vehement hatred at the very thought of his father. Merely brushing accidentally against his father's slacks, which were sometimes left hanging on the bathroom door, produced involuntary revulsion in Adam.

Adam was different from his brothers and cousins. During the Dark Time, the Adversary motivated many humans to view difference and individuality as unfavorable traits, despite assertions they made to the contrary. Humans tended to be conformists and felt uncomfortable with nonconformity. Difference often invited contempt. Being different was Adam's main offense, one for which he suffered severely.

The abuse Adam suffered at home and in school became so extreme, and his outlook so hopeless, that he came to hate his life. To avoid going to school, he would sometimes try to make himself sick by standing shirtless, outdoors in the winter cold, immediately after taking a hot bath. This strategy never worked for Adam. Adam hated his young life so intensely that he wished he could die, but death did not come—and he had not yet considered trying to expedite it.

Within about a year, Adam's father moved his family again and took them to a place known then as the Bronx, during one of the lowest points in the history of the area. Adam never forgot the night his family moved into their new Bronx apartment. Adam's father moved the furniture in earlier that day and took his family to their new apartment by night. He led his family up the dark stairs to a fifth-story apartment, Adam and his mother following behind.

This place was unlike Adam's Brooklyn apartment house with its well-lit, wide entranceway, high ceilings, clean walls, old European-style moldings, and black-and-white ceramic floor tiles. The stairway in this new building was poorly lit, dingy, and smelly, and the walls were dirty with a yellowish cast.

When they arrived at the landing of their fifth-floor apartment, Adam and his family were shocked by what they saw. Leaning against their door was a young man with a makeshift tourniquet around his arm, inserting a hypodermic needle into his vein. It was the first and only time Adam saw a heroin addict injecting himself. The drug addict greeted them nonchalantly and—in a friendly manner, as if engaged in a normal activity—welcomed them to the neighborhood. Adam's mother fainted in the stairwell before entering her new apartment.

Adam remained terrified of this strange and vile place as long as he lived there. He had heard, in school and on news programs, about people taking drugs and he had seen it in movies, but had never before actually witnessed it in real life.

In this new neighborhood, Adam witnessed many other things he had never seen before. He saw a violent crime committed just a few feet away from him, numerous fires, women selling their bodies to support addictions—visual evidence of the broken lives of people who had lost hope. He saw in their faces the physical signs of a spirit-crushing stress; a forlorn look of profound discouragement and humiliation, the effects of nearly perpetual indignity born out of generational oppression, poverty, war and diminished opportunities.

At times, Adam saw people in his neighborhood grieving for loved ones killed in a war that had been raging almost his entire life, though these same people were often treated, by the larger society, as foreigners with no stake in the country for which their loved ones fought and died.

Adam often saw young people loitering aimlessly, carousing or fighting. He saw people engaged in a constant pursuit of instant gratification and endless futile distractions, searching for relief from the pain and miserable meaninglessness of their lives.

But he also saw others holding tenaciously to high values, worthy principles and deep spiritual convictions, despite the stress they endured living in the chaos of their impoverished neighborhood. Those people rebuilt, restored, and repaired what others destroyed. They planted and tended trees, gardens, and seeds of hope for future generations.

Some of these people were members of his own family, including his mother. Even his father, contradictorily, held high values of morality in some areas of life, while treating his family with extreme and brutal harshness.

Adam's aunt, the wife of his father's brother, who was a veteran of what was called the Second World War, was a notable example of one who refused to allow herself and her family to be dragged into the morass that surrounded them.

On Adam's first day at his new school in the Bronx, two young men approached him as he walked out of the school building. He had been apprehensive about attending school in this dangerous neighborhood, and he felt relieved when he was approached in what seemed to be a friendly manner. Suddenly, one of the young men grabbed Adam and held an object he thought was a knife to his back. They forced Adam to a nearby park, where they took his brand-new leather jacket and all the money he had, a five-dollar bill, but they did not physically harm him.

It was cold and Adam was shivering as he walked with a shirt but no sweater or jacket. After walking a while, he noticed a young woman approaching him. He did not recognize her at first, but as they got closer to each other, he realized it was his cousin on her way home from classes at the university. He then realized he had walked a long distance in the wrong direction and was embarrassed.

But his cousin, a medical student several years older than Adam, was a compassionate person, a gentle soul with a kind face and peaceful demeanor. Adam admired her and loved her dearly, and would always remember her fondly. When she asked Adam what he was doing so far from home, he explained what had happened. His cousin took off her jacket, placed it over his shoulders, and escorted him home.

The Bronx neighborhood Adam's family had moved to was plagued with gang violence. The same week he had been robbed, while leaning against a car waiting for the school's opening bell, Adam saw a violent altercation erupt right near him. Some young men were chasing two other young men, one of whom tripped and fell barely fifty feet from where Adam was standing. Two of the gang members caught up with the one who had fallen. One pulled out a knife and plunged it into the fallen man's head. Never had Adam witnessed such extreme violence. Now, more than ever, Adam feared for his and his family's safety.

The family's next move took Adam to Brooklyn, to a small, neat apartment house in a clean, quiet area next door to the local police chief. The area immediately around Adam's new home was much nicer and safer than their previous neighborhood, but the larger region was almost as infested with drug-related crime and violence as their previous neighborhood. The new neighborhood was known as Sunset Park, a fitting name for an area in decline.

Once again, in this new neighborhood, Adam was mistreated by his peers. In fact, the contempt he faced in this new school was worse than anything he had previously experienced.

On his first day of school, Adam found himself walking through what seemed to be a gauntlet of hostile-looking teenage boys and girls glaring at him with angry stares. For a while Adam thought they would physically attack him. He could not understand why they displayed such antagonism toward someone they had never even seen before that moment. Seeing their antipathy toward him, Adam wondered if something was wrong with him. From that day forward, Adam was again subjected to insults, harassment and threats of violence at school. Not one of the students who mistreated Adam ever spoke to him otherwise. He wondered why they hated him. They seemed to have concluded that Adam was somehow inferior to them and felt justified in their persecution of him.

At this point in his life, Adam experienced something else he had never encountered before. For the first time in his life, he experienced overt racism.

He had been aware of racial tension in his country during his childhood and teenage years but, before moving to Sunset Park, had never been personally subjected to racially motivated abuse. Adam did not understand racism—or, for that matter, injustice or persecution of any sort. In his mind, all humans were members of the same family; just people struggling to survive together on the planet they all shared.

Adam's family was only one of two Hispanic families on his block. Soon after moving to this new neighborhood, a group of angry young men, much older than Adam, took to yelling out racial insults as he passed them on his way to school. It became a daily occurrence. As Adam approached the house in front of which they congregated, they would stick out their middle finger as they yelled out, "Spic!" Feeling increasingly threatened, Adam began taking a different and much longer route to school to avoid the daily morning insults.

Adam's father continued to move the family about once a year, until his death prevented him from doing so. After Adam's father's death, his mother continued moving the family frequently because of financial hardship. Adam became a perpetual newcomer; an outsider who was never able to establish roots or develop close friendships. He would often wander alone through dangerous areas in his new neighborhoods.

As Adam grew into adulthood, many of his choices, reactions, and patterns of thinking were born of fear, pain, and self-loathing. Indeed, profound disappointment, failure, and feelings of shame and guilt were so constant in his life that he came to expect nothing more, nothing better. Failure begat failure, causing Adam to always expect the same result. However, he held on tenaciously to the slightest glimmer of hope, as if it were a guiding light that would somehow, in a distant future or perhaps in another life, take him to a bright new world where his most cherished dreams would come true. But that was only a dream. Adam was certain that good things happened for him only in his dreams. Good things happened for other people, they happened in stories and in movies, but certainly not for him. His hopes were just dreams.

Adam's life was marked by an ongoing search for escape from emotional pain. He found some relief in music, which he loved and craved. He loved almost all forms of music, but was especially drawn to one genre then known as jazz. He also loved the sultry rhythms of his native Caribbean music, which he knew only as Latin music, as well rock, reggae, and European symphonic music.

When Adam was an adolescent, he tried learning to play the trumpet but did not pursue it enthusiastically. However, as a young man, he became captivated by the sound of the flute in modern jazz, fusion, and Caribbean music. Adam decided to learn to play this instrument. He attempted to teach himself to play the flute, and he was pleased to realize he had some musical ability. After attending a jazz workshop, one of the most fulfilling experiences he ever had, and taking private lessons, he became thoroughly absorbed in music.

Music became a new sanctuary for Adam, much as school had been when he was a child. But he soon found that, as one of his favorite musical artists once said, music eased but did not eliminate his pain. Eventually, the Malevolence made certain that Adam was introduced to alcohol and cannabis, and he started seeking solace in mind-altering escapes. He was unaware, of course, that he was actually succumbing to the treacherous grip of a heinous Malevolence bent on his destruction.

When Adam became a young adult, he moved into his own apartment. The insidious Malevolence moved in with him. During that time, Adam fell into a pit of depression and lost almost all hope. He continued attempting to alleviate the perpetual emotional pain with alcohol and cannabis. He had entirely lost his way on a dark path.

One day, while celebrating with co-workers after work, Adam drank too much alcohol and became drunk. He fell asleep on the train on his way home. After some time, Adam realized he had slept past his stop and gone all the way to the end of the line; which was well past his home. He fell asleep again. It was very late and no other passengers were on the train. A police officer saw Adam sleeping and ordered him off the train. He was forced off the train in the heart of the city. Adam sat on a park bench and again started dosing off. After a few minutes, he got up and started staggering toward the subway station. A group of young people, who also seemed intoxicated, saw him stumbling and tried to help him get into the subway station safely. Unbeknownst to Adam, Mikhael, his Guardian, was among them.

Adam struggled to get money out of his pocket to buy a subway token, but some of it began falling out. Disguised as a human, Mikhael approached him and said, "Hey man, you're gonna lose your money." He tucked Adam's money in his pocket and helped him into the subway station and onto the train. Mikhael entered the train with Adam, resumed his invisible form, and made sure he arrived home safely.

When Adam got home, he fell face down as he was approaching the steps to his apartment. As Adam lay on his face, a mandate went out from the Infinite Realm.

"Mikhael, lift him up. This is beneath his dignity and does not reflect his destiny. It is time to remove the veil from his eyes. Awaken him."

Mikhael lifted Adam and enabled him to stumble into his apartment. Besides the exhaustion of a long workday, the effects of cannabis and alcohol had thoroughly dulled Adam's mind. He was weary of numbing his senses trying to find relief from the overwhelming depression and hopelessness that were choking him.

He was weary of pondering the possible meaning of his miserable existence. He cringed in disgust as he looked at his image in his bathroom mirror. He went to bed depressed and soon fell into a deep stupor.

* * * * * *

Adam began to stir restlessly as he slept and then suddenly awoke. He knew he had fallen asleep and was sure he was now fully awake, but he did not recognize his surroundings. In fact, Adam felt he had somehow awakened inside of what seemed to be an incredibly surreal dream. Yet it was not a dream. It was more real than anything he had ever experienced.

In the Infinite Realm, a Guardian of the Portals approached an Elder of the Council about a matter of urgency. "My Lord, an intruder from the space-time continuum approaches the main portal leading to the Great Hall."

The Elder responded, "It is the Adversary."

The Guardian recalled fierce battles he had personally fought to repel the Adversary and his army of rebels during the great war that raged at the inception of the Dark Time. In a fraction of an Earth-moment, the entire Guard of the Portal prepared to engage the Adversary in a confrontation. The Guardian asked the Elder, "Sir, shall we deny access?"

The Elder replied, "No. He is a ruler. So long as he approaches in peace regarding a matter of protocol or judicial concern, he must be granted access, but only to the Great Hall."

Despite his rebellion, the Adversary was allowed limited access to the Realm because of his position. Though exiled, he remained de facto ruler over the Earth and its atmosphere. However, no evil entity, regardless of position, was allowed to enter the Realm outside the confines of the Great Hall.

The Adversary approached the Great Hall, and stood upon the crystal platform that hovered in front of and somewhat below the main portal. He waited for the customary procedure to transpire.

The Guardian addressed the Adversary: "State your business. What do you seek?"

The Adversary responded, "An audience with the Council regarding a judicial matter."

The Guardian protested, "Do you not know that your presence is unwelcomed in this place?"

In naked arrogance, the Adversary hissed, "I am a reigning monarch—"

The Guardian interrupted abruptly, "—of a despotic kingdom limited by space and time and slated for inevitable demise. You are an exiled rebel. However, you are granted an audience. Proceed with caution."

The Council of Elders immediately convened. The members of the Council took their places. They knew this proceeding would affect the life and destiny of a certain human, one who had been named by his parents Adan de Las Aguas, but was known as Adam by all who knew him on Earth. Judgment would be rendered on matters of transcendent importance.

The Chief Elder addressed the Adversary: "State your purpose."

The Adversary responded with unveiled arrogance, "Permission to destroy the little human."

Unmoved by the Adversary's contempt, the Elder asked, "On what grounds?"

"His life is mine by right."

"What is the basis for your claim?"

"He has forfeited his life of his own free will."

"How so?"

"By choosing the path that leads to the destruction of his species."

In a dimension outside time and space, a human life will hang in the balance, in a mysterious trial before a tribunal who will weigh the evidence and render a verdict.

Chapter 11

Verdict

"Present your case."

In the Infinite Realm, a Watcher addressed the Adversary.

At the center of the Great Hall, hovered a mysterious device, an enormous object with wheels within other wheels, constantly spinning at incredible speeds and emanating colored lights—brilliant white, variations of blue, green, red, and a color like that of burning coals. Flashes of lightning proceeded from it. To humans, the appearance of this strange wonder might have been reminiscent of the atom.

However, the strangest aspect of this phenomenon is that this device was not merely an inanimate object as it seemed. Rather, it is a living thing with a life that originated in the most ancient reality, well before the inception of space-time, a life that exists even now and will continue throughout eternity.

The wheels contain part of the life essence or consciousness of the most powerful Luminous Beings who have an exalted position attending the Majestic Throne of all realities. These high-ranking beings would, at times, enter the space-time continuum as entourage of the Infinite Mind. The spokes of the mysterious wheels are completely covered by what appear to be eyes that emit the multicolored lights. Most humans would have considered this marvel a freakish sight. However, the eyes of the wheels-within-wheels contain and project images of every object and every being in every moment in time, as if they had recorded all events that ever occurred in the space-time continuum.

During a proceeding in the Great Hall, any being could extract images from the whirling wheels-within-wheels to be used as evidence in a case. In an instant, the Adversary appeared in the center of the Hall and touched the whirling wheels. With a sliding motion of one finger, as humans would swipe an icon on a cellular telephone, he caused the man called Adam to appear in the Great Hall. Adam appeared in the flesh, as real as his literal existence on Earth.

* * * * * *

After falling into a deep sleep and suddenly finding himself wide awake again, Adam seemed to have been transported to a mysterious otherworldly place. He had no idea where he had been taken or who had taken him there, yet Adam knew he was no longer on Earth, but in another world. He was not in a vessel of any kind, but he had the sense that he was being transported at an incredible speed—faster than the speed of light, if that were possible.

As he soared through this world, Adam caught glimpses of extraordinary landscapes that seemed to extend endlessly with no visible horizon. He was amazed that he was able to see things clearly at what seemed to be incredibly far distances. Suddenly, he was rocketed toward an incredibly tall mountain, the top of which was completely shrouded by blinding bright light. Adam stared at the light and after a few moments found that he could not see.

Fearing he had been blinded, he instinctively covered his eyes, but after a few minutes he regained his eyesight and was able to look directly at the bright light with no discomfort. Never had Adam seen such brilliant lights and mystifying wonders.

Adam was now in what seemed to be a city and approaching a beautiful but very strange building. Suddenly, without walking through any entrance, Adam found himself inside the building. Adam was filled with wonder as well as fear.

Since he felt completely awake, Adam wondered how this could possibly be a dream. Little did he know that he had been extracted from his world and taken to another dimension by the Adversary. Adam wondered, "*Where am I?*" He had been taken to the Great Hall where the Council had convened. The Hall was beautiful in a strange way. It was unlike anything Adam had ever seen. The place was magnificent, and the beings in it were imposing. The entire experience was so overwhelming that Adam was left speechless.

But his awe quickly turned to fear. Adam could not see his captors, but he felt physically restrained and as if he were being dragged. He felt hard, cold metal around his wrists and ankles and heard the clanking sound of chains, but could not see the invisible chains that bound him. Confused by this bizarre experience, Adam began to panic.

Adam was being brought before some sort of tribunal of alien-looking beings. Although some of the beings had recognizably human features, others bore no resemblance whatsoever to humans. He started to wonder if he had been abducted by aliens.

Overwhelmed with confusion and terror, Adam listened intently. He had never been so alert in his life. Every muscle in his body was tense. He then had a disturbing thought. Perhaps he had died and was about to face the eternal judgment about which his parents had so often warned him and his siblings. Adam was convinced that if he had died, he would surely be sent to the place of eternal torment his parents called hell.

Adam's knees and bowels weakened. He felt like he might soon collapse and slip into unconsciousness.

Instead of being placed in a chair, as he would have expected had he been in an earthly courtroom, Adam was placed inside what appeared to be a clear cone. The cone sat on top of a glowing disc that floated in the midst of a circle of twenty-four gleaming thrones upon which sat his judges. The thrones began orbiting around Adam as if they were planets and he was the sun. Everything in this strange place seemed to fly, hover, or spin around.

A proceeding of some sort began. Adam could not hear any words being spoken, but somehow was able to understand everything being communicated. He perceived that he and his life were being discussed. The beings in the tribunal kept using a term he understood only as *the Man*, but Adam knew he was "the Man" to whom they referred.

One being, with a terrifying appearance, a grotesque creature, seemed to be prosecuting Adam before the tribunal. This creature repeatedly referred to Adam with obvious contempt. He did not refer to Adam by his name or as "the Man" as the other beings did. He would refer to Adam merely as "the human" or "the little organic creature." Though Adam had no way of knowing it, the prosecutor was his lifelong nemesis, the Adversary.

The prosecutor seemed intent on presenting Adam in the most unfavorable light. Adam understood that he was being depicted as utterly corrupt and hopelessly flawed. The prosecutor insisted that Adam had spurned the unique potential for which he had been destined and, as such, was unworthy of life in the Infinite Realm. Adam wondered what this talk about a unique destiny and life in an Infinite Realm meant. Was the prosecutor referring to the afterlife he had heard about since he was a child? Then, utterly confused, he thought to himself, "Maybe I *am* dead!"

The tribunal continued their discussion about Adam. Strangely, it now seemed that the members of the tribunal were expressing sympathy toward Adam. A dialogue ensued between the Adversary and the tribunal. Some members of the Council asserted that Adam's deficiencies, which made him prone to transgressing the Infinite Laws, resulted from conditioning under the Adversary's constant, lifelong oppression. They said he had been blinded by the Adversary's deception and that he was not yet aware of certain realities. They stated that, since Adam was not yet able to clearly see the paths available to him and fully appreciate the consequences of the choices he made, he could not be said to have made a choice at all.

Again, Adam wondered what they were referring to. *Just what was he blind to?*

Adam did not realize that he was indeed blind; blind to the purpose of what seemed to him a meaningless life and hopeless existence. He lived in a daze, a hopeless cycle of negative emotions, actions, and reactions.

Suddenly, Adam felt that he was free of the shackles with which he had been bound and no longer inside the invisible cone. He now seemed to be a spectator, watching strange events unfold like a dream within a dream. But now the alien-looking beings seemed to be totally ignoring or no longer seeing him.

What happened next held Adam transfixed. He saw himself, as if he were watching a movie in which he played the lead role. But he did not appear as a recorded image or a hologram. He was real. Adam saw himself in flesh and blood, confused, terrified, and walking awkwardly as if he were being pulled along. Adam heard the sound of a chain, but just as before, he could not see it. It seemed like he was watching a recording of what he had just experienced.

He watched as his other self was placed inside what appeared to be a glass cone, hovering in the center of the Hall exactly the way he had been just a short while earlier. The other Adam threw himself violently against the wall of the invisible cone in a frustrated attempt to escape. Suddenly, the Adam in the cone stopped and stared directly at Adam. Adam instantly felt chills as if he had seen a fearful sight. The two Adams stared at each other intently for a brief moment. Seeing himself in the cone, being relentlessly prosecuted, Adam was awakened to the reality of another self who lived contrary to the values he held dear, or at least wanted to hold dear.

Adam felt compelled to move closer to get a better look. Hoping he would not be noticed, he walked slowly and quietly toward the area where this bizarre scene was taking place.

That he was able to walk at all was strange, because there was no floor. Instead, Adam seemed to be walking through space. He could see what looked like distant galaxies and stars with planets orbiting around them. After walking only a few feet forward, Adam ran into an invisible barrier of some sort. At first, he thought it was an invisible wall, but then he realized it was something else. When he extended his hands to explore what was preventing him from moving forward, he was surprised to feel—not a wall, but bars.

Adam followed the invisible bars until he ended up right back where he had started. He realized that, though he had been released from the chains that had been restraining him, he was now inside an invisible cell. It seemed to be a very small cell, with an area of only about three or four square feet.

Disappointed about his new confinement, Adam began walking backward. Strangely, the invisible cell seemed to move with him wherever he went, as if it were a portable prison cell. He was able to walk backward, to the left and right without being obstructed, but he could walk forward for only a short distance.

Adam saw the grotesque being he thought must be the prosecutor orbiting around his other self, apparently enjoying the frustration of the man trapped inside the cone and his vain efforts to escape. The prosecutor had a terrifying, intimidating presence and an aggressive demeanor. He was enraged and exuded a hatred that was almost palpable to Adam. His rage appeared to be directed not just at Adam, but at the beings in the court as well.

Adam then saw a large scale with two balances. As the proceeding continued, the Adversary recited a detailed list of Adam's dysfunctions and misdeeds in embarrassing detail. The Adversary proceeded to present evidence in the form of a three-dimensional video of some sort. Adam was amazed but his amazement quickly turned to shame as he watched his indiscretions displayed openly before these alien beings. But their interest seemed to be only in the judicial aspects of the evidence presented and not in the sordid details the Adversary wanted to focus their attention on.

Strangely, as if he were observing another person's plight rather than his own, Adam felt sympathy for his other self, who lowered his head in shame as the video streamed. Adam observed his other self being tried for lifelong infractions of some universal code of behavior of which he knew nothing.

Adam then saw a remarkable wonder. As the prosecutor recounted each of his offenses and moral deficiencies, every indiscretion and habitual selfish act, a fine dust suddenly appeared above the scales and began falling on one of the balances. At first, it looked like the fine powdery sand of an hourglass. But as the dust accumulated, piling up layer upon layer, something began to take shape. The dust began to crystallize into a figure, as if a statue was being formed in front of Adam's eyes.

At first, Adam could not recognize what it was. He then saw clearly what looked like two human feet, followed by ankles, then legs, a torso, chest, and arms. In amazement, Adam realized that a human body was being created out of dust. He looked at his other self and saw that, as the human shape was taking form on the other side of the scale, his other self was gradually disappearing from the cone. With intense curiosity, Adam stared as the Adversary continued his litany of offenses until the neck, head, and face were finally formed on the other side of the scale.

Adam was stupefied. It was his own body he saw being formed and now saw standing on the other side of the balance. He wondered in confusion, "What does this mean?" Adam, mistakenly, assumed what he saw confirmed what he had always believed: he was the sum total of his deficiencies. But, it was nothing more than a creative deception contrived by the Adversary.

The Adversary whirled fiendishly around the balance where the other Adam stood with his head hung in shame. With an accusatory finger, he shone a reddish light on Adam's naked body and with an openly-sarcastic laugh, said, "Behold, the man."

The Beings in the tribunal suddenly rose from their thrones and for a brief moment looked intently at the pitiful man on the scale. They then turned their backs, and vanished. The trial seemed to have reached a strangely inconclusive end. No verdict had been proclaimed. Adam thought, *"Is this how trials are conducted here? Perhaps a formal verdict is not needed. Maybe it's just understood."* Adam's heart sank as he concluded that he must have been found guilty and would, most likely, have to pay the ultimate penalty, which must surely be death.

However, Adam was still perplexed and kept wondering why no verdict had been formally read. From what he had seen, these beings seemed to follow the strictest protocols. *"How could a trial end without a verdict being formally proclaimed?"* Moreover, Adam had a strange feeling that the tribunal was saddened, apparently disappointed by the flagrant display of his dysfunctions and failures. Before the judges disappeared, he had thought, or rather, had hoped, they were reluctant to impose the death penalty. However, the prosecutor did not appear willing to accept a lesser punishment.

Then a being with a metallic glow and movements that seemed almost mechanical appeared and approached Adam's other self. The being seemed to radiate heat. He was not gargantuan, but he was extremely imposing. His very person seemed to be a weapon of destruction.

Adam's other self quickly moved back and fell to a fetal position as if bracing himself for a violent attack. With a deep voice that caused Adam's legs to weaken, the being addressed Adam's other self, "Human, how do you plead?" No anger was evident in his voice. In fact, the being expressed no emotion at all. It seemed that he merely wanted to enter an official plea. It seemed rather strange to Adam for a plea to be entered at the end, rather than the beginning, of a trial.

The Adversary objected vehemently, "Why ask for his plea? His guilt is without question."

The glowing being's demeanor suddenly changed. Glowing even brighter, he turned toward the Adversary with focused indignation and responded, "Though you do not allow it in your domain, protocols in the Infinite Realm require that all conscious beings be allowed an opportunity to choose and enter a plea."

The Watcher then turned his attention back to Adam's other self and repeated his question. "Human, how do you plead?"

Adam's other self stared nervously at the being questioning him without answering a word. The Watcher asked a third time, now with more intensity, "Human, how do you plead?" Adam broke down in grief as he watched. How else could he plead? He knew he was guilty. It was incontrovertible.

Suddenly, Adam found himself in total darkness. He heard a voice that was strangely familiar to him. He recognized the voice. He had heard it all his life but had never been able to associate it with a face or with any person he knew. The voice was the Adversary's.

The Adversary berated Adam, "Well, how do you plead, human?"

Adam remained silent.

"Did you think your life was all a game and that there would never be a reckoning? For years, you read to yourself and wrote the words of Moses in your journal, 'Lord, teach us to number our days, that we may gain a heart of wisdom.' But you never did gain that heart of wisdom, did you? Oh, and did you think there would be someone here to defend you, to plead your case? Were you, perhaps, expecting a defense attorney to be assigned to your case?"

The prosecutor laughed in derision.

"This is not Earth. By the way, where is that deity you sometimes prayed to? I guess he's not here. I don't see him. Do you? So, how do you plead? You are guilty and hopelessly corrupt, but their stupid laws are so unfair. I would fight them if I were you. If you plead guilty, they will just execute you. There is no mercy here. Fight them!"

Adam was acutely aware of his guilt. "*What point is there in a trial?*", he wondered. He would have had nothing to say in his defense, even if he were allowed to speak, which did not seem would be the case. Besides, no one had taken up his defense. Apparently, he was indefensible. Adam was confused. It was evident that the prosecutor sought the death penalty, yet he was advising him to proclaim his innocence and defend himself. Adam thought briefly about the possibility of pleading not guilty, but quickly realized he faced overwhelming and irrefutable evidence that proved his guilt. The evidence presented was not in the form of a mere video recording that could be doctored or edited as sometimes occurred on Earth. There would be no question about perspective, no debate about evidence taken out of context. The events were presented as they had happened.

There was no opportunity to plea bargain or appeal, as he might have been able to do in an earthly court. Adam feared pleading not guilty might actually make his situation worse. He wondered if he then would be found guilty of and punished for an additional, perhaps worse, infraction—that is, lying to an extraterrestrial tribunal. He held onto a hope that if he pleaded guilty and threw himself on the mercy of the court, he might receive leniency from his judges.

Adam found himself again in the Great Hall as if no time at all had elapsed. Overwhelmed by the weight of his guilt, Adam broke down in grief as he watched his other self being interrogated. How else could he plead? He knew he was guilty. It was incontrovertible. Adam and his other self simultaneously fell to their knees in profound contrition. In perfect unison, they proclaimed before the tribunal, "I am guilty."

Then Adam heard an ominous sound, which he thought sealed his fate. The prosecutor shrieked, "He has entered his plea. He has confessed his guilt! Deliver him to me!"

The Watcher who had approached Adam's other self for his plea flew toward a podium made of gleaming white marble. The podium sat on a platform with the appearance of black onyx. The Watcher, glowing as burning coals, walked up to the podium on what appeared to be floating stone steps. As he walked up the steps, each stone touched by his feet would burst into fiery luminescence. The Watcher unfurled a scroll on which he wrote with a glowing quill.

As he addressed the Council, his thunderous voice rumbled through the hall, causing the pillars to shake as he said, "Let it be known that the man has confessed his guilt. By virtue of the evidence presented and by his own admission, he is guilty. Unless another accepts his penalty, protocol demands that he suffer the penalty he has earned—death."

Suddenly, with a wave of the Watcher's hand, a portal opened on one side of the hall. In an instant, Adam saw himself transported through the portal to yet another dimension, where a horde of hideous creatures approached the scale on which was standing the other Adam. Adam concluded that these foul creatures were the executioners. He watched as they mounted the platform and apprehended his other self. The creatures were vile and bloodthirsty, nothing like the elegant Luminous Beings of the tribunal.

After the reading of the verdict and the sentencing, the Great Hall had temporarily become darkened by the dense fog surrounding the Adversary.

After a few moments, the Watcher behind the white marble podium glowed even more brilliantly in the darkened hall than before. Now all the Watchers glowed more brightly. Their brilliance quickly overcame the darkness and once again lit up the hall. Adam saw the members of the tribunal, sitting on their thrones, which were now arranged in a circle around the podium. The prosecutor was also there.

Adam thought the proceeding had concluded with his apparent sentencing, but the Watcher at the podium motioned toward a scroll that, throughout the proceeding, had remained floating directly above a stone pedestal. The scroll immediately flew into his hand and unfurled.

Opening the scroll, the Watcher addressed the Adversary in a deep and powerful voice. "Although the man has confessed his guilt, no conscious being is to be condemned in the Infinite Realm without an advocate. The man must have an advocate. It is protocol."

Adam wondered at this strange turn of events, *"Why would an attorney be assigned after a guilty verdict has already been proclaimed?"* As if to confirm the Watcher's words, a light shone through a section of the scroll, which Adam concluded must contain the rules of protocol.

The protocol was clear. Adam did not know who would possibly advocate for him, but the being proclaimed it: he was to have an advocate.

Chapter 12

The Advocate

At that moment, another being whom Adam had not seen before appeared and the configuration of the Great Hall again changed. The being's throne was now in the center of the hall, set upon a great platform that had the appearance of a massive emerald. All other thrones in the Hall were instantly rearranged in a semicircle around the gleaming platform.

Immediately, all the Luminous Beings rose and knelt on both knees in an obvious display of deference, then resumed their positions on their thrones. Even the Adversary knelt, but more out of fear and pretense than the reverence shown by the others. His was not the same demeanor as that of the Luminous Beings. He was a defeated but defiant and resentful rebel, an avowed adversary, as his name aptly described.

Adam was awed by the sight of this being, whom he concluded must be the ruler of this mysterious place. This being was, in some ways, similar to the others in the Great Hall, but obviously superior to them. He was incredibly majestic. His very presence commanded deference. When Adam felt the gaze of his piercing eyes, he knew with certainty that the depths of his being had been thoroughly inspected. Every thought and feeling were exposed to this being.

All of the beings in the tribunal radiated light, but this other being appeared to be literally composed of and wrapped in incredibly dazzling, almost blinding light. When sitting on his throne, which was magnificent, but fearsome when it emitted lightning, his body appeared to be engulfed in flames from his waist down.

As the being rose from his throne, everyone in the Great Hall instantly stood on their feet. Then Adam saw a most curious sight. With every step the being took, light would shine under what appeared to be his feet and crystallize into a portable platform, similar to the emerald platform over which his throne hovered.

As Adam stared at this being, he heard the words Infinite Mind in his mind as if the being were introducing himself.

The Infinite Mind addressed the Council and the Adversary: "I will serve as the man's advocate."

Adam wondered what could be more incredible. Despite his obvious guilt and profound dysfunction, Adam was being defended by none other than one who appeared to be a ruler, perhaps the supreme ruler, of this mysterious place. After fearing that he was facing certain death, Adam now began to feel hopeful. But why would this apparent ruler advocate for him? Then, almost as in response to Adam's question, a wave of images, thoughts, and feelings flooded his mind. Immediately, Adam felt emotionally overwhelmed. He saw the forlorn faces of many people, some of whom he had known throughout his life and others he had never met. He somehow knew that all these people were broken and hopeless, and that his experiences were somehow connected to them. Adam felt as if he was no longer living his own life but was instead experiencing the lives of other humans, all of whom were bound by unseen shackles and experiencing excruciating suffering.

He became a young man suffering with mental illness, trapped within a prison in his own mind. Adam did not just *see* this person—he *became* him. He became a young child afflicted with debilitating physical impairments. He experienced several physical and emotional disabilities: leprosy, blindness, and AIDS. He became crippled, a prisoner, an orphan.

Adam felt their pain, the physical as well as the emotional suffering that resulted from the rejection they experienced. He felt the agony of an unmarried mother struggling in poverty while being the target of scathing criticism. Adam experienced the aching loneliness of a poor immigrant, far from home and separated from family, trying to survive in a foreign land. He became a terrified refugee fleeing horrific violence, seeking asylum in countries that mistrusted his intentions, and hated him merely because of his physical appearance.

In one strange moment, Adam became old, alone, poor and forgotten. He sorrowed deeply seeing accomplishments he had wrought over a lifetime overlooked; cast by a calloused society upon a heap of trifles. He experienced childhood physical and sexual abuse. He found himself addicted to drugs and alcohol, a slave to tyrannical cravings. He was overwhelmed by the excruciating heartache of a young man rejected by his wife for the attention of other men, and by the anguish of a woman battered by verbal, emotional, and physical abuse, and then abandoned by her husband. He felt the sting of loss caused by broken promises, and grieved the death of hope, and much, much more.

Each of the lives he experienced was singular and unique, yet all became one in Adam. Adam wondered if his purpose was to bear witness to others, who felt hopeless as he did, that they too had a powerful advocate, despite all appearances to the contrary in their reality.

When the Infinite Mind declared that he would serve as his advocate, Adam was moved to the core of his being both by the effect of the words and by the very sound of the voice that uttered them. The force emitted by the Infinite Mind's voice terrified Adam. The voice was like a booming echo going right through Adam's being. It sounded like several deep voices speaking in perfect unison. It was a deep, thunderous sound and felt like waves of energy that shook both his physical body and his mind. As Adam felt this tsunami of energy surge through him, he remembered images of atomic weapons exploding. He wanted to hide, but had nowhere to run. He fell into a fetal position, with his hands clasped around his head.

After a few moments, Adam composed himself enough to be able to again look at the Advocate. However, the Adversary instantly caused Adam to return to the space-time continuum, back to Earth. The appearance of the Infinite Mind to act as Adam's advocate was a terribly inconvenient turn of events for the Adversary.

He objected manipulatively, "Far be it from me to accuse you of injustice, but how is advocating for a transgressor of the universal laws you implemented and by which you hold all conscious beings accountable justice? The little human has made his choice and entered his guilty plea. Sentencing is a mere formality. There is no need for lengthening the proceeding."

Addressing the Adversary, the Infinite Mind asserted that Adam had not been fully aware of the implications of his actions. He had been coerced and not allowed by the Adversary to make a free choice. Therefore, he could not be forced to pay the penalty.

The Adversary protested insolently, "*I* have not allowed him? Is it not *you* who restricts his freedom with your many commands? Is it not *you* who *commands* him concerning what to do and what not to do? I do not restrict his liberty. On the contrary, I provide opportunity for him to grasp what he naturally craves."

The Advocate responded, "Have you not oppressed him since birth, as you have also done to many generations of his ancestors, thwarting his ability to choose wisely from the time he opened his organic eyes? He has not yet had an opportunity to choose freely."

* * * * * * *

Indeed, several generations of Adam's ancestors had suffered under the relentless oppression of an unseen, evil Adversary. Some of Adam's ancestors had been immigrants who had left their native lands in search of better opportunities. Others fled their homes because of religious or political persecution.

Both of Adam's parents were descendants of Sephardim, who had fled for safety after the infamous Alhambra Decree. When the Catholic monarch of Spain issued the Edict of Expulsion on March 31, 1492, all Jews were expelled from the Kingdoms of Castile and Aragon. Some fled to what was then known as the New World, where they changed or concealed anything that could identify them as Jews. Many took new names related to places they hailed from or to their professions. For generations, they practiced their faith in secret, at the risk of dire consequences, including torture and death, if discovered. Eventually their children and children's children relinquished the memories, traditions, and faith of their fathers.

Some of Adam's ancestors, people indigenous to the areas the Spaniards had conquered, were brought to near extinction through oppressive slave labor, violence, and disease. A few fled to the thick jungles and mountainous areas of Adam's native isle, but after much intermarriage, they were no longer a distinct group. The rest of Adam's ancestors were Africans brought to his Caribbean island as slaves after most of the indigenous natives were decimated.

After losing ownership of the land their ancestors had lived on and tilled for generations, the families of Adam's father and mother fell into grinding poverty. Adam's father was born to a poor family in the early days of what humans then called the twentieth century. Adam's grandfather, Don Domingo Cruz, was a violent and impulsive plantation foreman, full of rage and feared by all. Armed with a handgun and a machete, which he used as both a tool and a weapon, he rode up and down the plantation on a large white stallion he called Napoleon.

Inflamed by lust, Don Domingo, Adam's grandfather, took his wife's younger sister, who was only fourteen years old, as his concubine. When he was a young boy, Adam heard his father tell a bizarre story about this young girl who became his grandmother.

When his young concubine became pregnant with Adam's father, Don Domingo, ironically, accused her of infidelity. Intent on killing the young girl, Adam's grandfather put his pistol to her head and prepared to shoot her. But just as he was about to pull the trigger, Adam's father, a newborn babe only nine days old, cried out, "Papa, no!" Don Domingo fearfully put away his weapon. Never again did he threaten Adam's grandmother with violence.

When Adam's father was about eight years old, Don Domingo was conscripted into the First World War, which, ironically, humans also called "The War to End All Wars." It was a horrible conflict in which more than sixteen million lives were lost. His grandfather never came back from this war, and at the age of nine, Adam's father was forced to work in the sugarcane fields to help support his family.

His formal education ended after fifth grade; nevertheless, he came to possess a formidable intellect and developed an excellent command of spoken and written Spanish. He would read newspaper articles in English and translate them instantaneously into perfect Spanish. He read widely about many different topics, including politics, history, religion, and science, and composed several pieces of music and poetry.

Adam's father witnessed many pivotal historical events. Adam remembered his father reminiscing about the first two World Wars and the Great Depression. Sometimes, when Adam's father would talk about the first of the three World Wars waged by humans, he would sing, in his heavily accented English, American and British patriotic war songs he had learned as a young boy. He often shared memories of his experiences during the Great Depression, a time when many people suffered great financial hardship.

Often, when food was scarce in the house, he would speak about a time that he and some friends were so famished, they roasted and ate a cat. A friend of Adam's father, a blind man he remembered seeing in his neighborhood when he was a young boy, would walk over one of the bridges from Brooklyn into Manhattan to collect food thrown in the garbage after wealthy patrons had dined.

Adam's father was raised in a world of darkness, a reality saturated in superstition. When he was a young child, he inherited a mantle passed on from his father, Don Domingo, who had inherited it from Adam's great-grandmother. As a young man, he became an avid student of the dark arts and a disciple of a well-known American clairvoyant and eventually became known in his community as a powerful sorcerer. He plunged deeper into darkness, until one day he completely lost his memory. For an entire year, he did not know who he was. Adam's father's mind and spirit were impacted so profoundly, that he never fully recovered from the negative effects he suffered.

Adam remembered how, as a child, he would hear his father, in the middle of the night, contending with and chasing evil spirits through their apartment. He would sometimes hear his father, in pursuit of an evil spirit he thought he had seen, stomping down the hall and yelling, "*Sin verguenza!* Se metio alli." ("Shameless one! He hid there.") Adam would cover his head with his blanket in fear.

The Malevolence had also oppressed Adam's mother, who had been abandoned twice by her mother. The first time was during the early days of the Great Depression, when she was barely three years old. Her mother left her husband and children for a life with a wealthy land-owning Spaniard. Subsequently, Adam's mother's father took his young daughter to live with his mother on a farm in a mountainous region of their tropical island. Even at that tender age, the little girl loved her father dearly and longed to be with him. She spoke lovingly of her father her entire life.

When Adam's mother was about ten years of age, her mother reentered her life and attempted to reconnect with her. She would take her young daughter on visits to the ranch where she and her new husband lived. They had a beautiful home, several guesthouses, and livestock of all sorts—herds of cattle, pigs, goats, and chickens. Mesmerized by the abundance and opulence enjoyed by her mother, half-siblings, and step-siblings, Adam's mother eventually decided to leave her grandmother's farm and go live with her mother. One night, she quietly slipped out of her grandmother's home and walked alone down the dark mountain path. She was afraid, but her desire for a better life exceeded her fear. She proceeded cautiously down the dark trail, comforted by the melodious, birdlike chirps of coquis, small tree frogs native to her island. She finally made her way safely to her stepfather's ranch.

It was a new world to her, a fanciful world with rolling acres of luscious greenery, beautiful palm trees, manicured gardens and obvious opulence tended by field workers and servants. Near the center of the property was the family's large home, where they enjoyed luxuries largely unknown even in the powerful nation that controlled her native island. One of the guesthouses served as quarantine quarters for one of her half-brothers, who was dying of tuberculosis, a highly contagious disease.

Soon after arriving at her step-father's ranch, Adam's mother suffered a great disillusionment. To her surprise, she was received not as a daughter, but as a servant and nurse for her half-brother, whom she came to love dearly. She never regretted caring for him, and often spoke about how he died in her arms. But, the indignity she suffered, treated as a lowly and expendable servant in her own mother's home, caused her profound pain.

Adam's mother quickly saw how differently she was treated as compared to the children of her Spanish stepfather. Though she had only been able to attend school for two years in her entire life, she was not sent to school. In contrast, her half-siblings, were sent to European universities and became accomplished professionals and business owners. Eventually, she was subjected to another insidious indignity at her mother's home. It was the worst humiliation she had ever experienced. Her stepfather, who was a vile man of whom she lived in constant fear, attempted to sexually assault her when she was a young girl.

For a time, it seemed there would be no end to the humiliations she suffered in this new world. She was not born in this opulent world and the inhabitants thereof never let her forget she was not one of their own. She was the impoverished child of a former marriage and viewed as not much more than a lowly servant. One incident wounded her so deeply that she never forgot the event and would speak of it many years later, even after having had children of her own.

One day, while sitting in a hospital waiting room with her mother, siblings, and half-siblings, a woman asked her mother if they were all her children. Her mother gestured with her hand only toward the children she bore to her wealthy Spanish husband and responded, "*These* are all my children." This was not lost on Adam's mother. It was painfully apparent to her that her mother intentionally excluded her and her siblings; the mulatto children from her previous marriage, effectively denying them. Though she forgave her mother, this painful rejection affected her for the rest of her life.

A few years later, she was abandoned a second time. Her mother, stepfather, and half-siblings temporarily left the ranch and moved away without her. She was a young girl; alone, afraid, and homeless. The heartbreaking realization that she really was no more than an expendable servant to her mother and stepfather was brought home to her in a painful manner.

Fortunately, she was able to move in with one of her brothers and his wife, but provisions were scarce during that time and they were struggling to feed themselves. Soon after Adam's mother moved in, her sister-in-law put a lock on the food pantry. Adam's mother was so hungry that she began feeding on whatever tubercles, staples in their native diet, she could find growing wild in the fields, even before they had fully ripened.

It was a harsh existence, but the Watchers ensured her survival and guarded the core of her spirit, for she was to be the mother of a bridge for the fourth generation. Adam's generation was the fourth since the Realm's last major intervention in the history of his family. According to protocol, the Infinite Realm would intervene in order to prevent the passing of the mantle of darkness to the fifth generation.

Although protocol demands accountability for choices made freely by conscious beings, a delicate balance must be maintained in a universe where this freedom is allowed. Freedom must be balanced against the possibility of universal chaos or the wholesale oppression of the weak by the strong. The cycle of evil must be interrupted every third or fourth generation so as to avoid an imbalance that could result in the loss of all freedom.

Adam was to be a bridge over which many would cross from bondage to freedom. He would be shielded from the worst effects of evil in order to provide him an opportunity to freely choose or reject his destiny. Several others in the fourth generation would be chosen as instruments of change to pave the way for future generations and maintain universal balance. However, they were all completely unaware of the destiny for which they had been chosen and prepared.

Adam's mother and grandmother eventually reestablished and maintained contact, but much damage had been done to their relationship. Adam's grandmother, without actually expressing remorse, made efforts in later years to compensate for abandoning her daughter. She regularly provided food for Adam's mother and her children while his father was working overseas. However, the effects of being abandoned, rejected, humiliated, and abused resulted in deep emotional scars in Adam's mother. These scars were inherited by her children and taken advantage of by the Malevolence.

Indeed, her children inherited negative traits from three generations of Adam's ancestors who had been relentlessly oppressed and bound by unseen entities who had been exiled to Earth ages before any of them were born.

* * * * * * *

"You may touch him, but you may not destroy him. He has a special destiny." In the Infinite Realm, Adam's Advocate addressed the Adversary.

The Adversary wanted to do more than merely touch Adam. He wanted to utterly annihilate him. He was curious about Adam's destiny. With unveiled arrogance, he responded, "You say he has a special destiny, yet you also claim you have granted him the ability to freely choose his path. Does not one negate the other? Or will you extract his allegiance by force, as you accuse me of doing?"

The Adversary relished the idea of forcing the human to follow his path. He excelled at coercion and force. The Adversary continued, "Do you not see he is hopelessly flawed and naturally prone to faltering? He has already chosen his path." He let out a condescending laugh, and added, "They live in houses of clay and are slaves to the impulses of their biological chemistry. He will bring about his own destruction."

"He will falter and he will fall," agreed the Advocate. "However, I will sustain him. When he falls, I will lift him up. He has not yet chosen freely."

The Adversary insisted, "He will eventually fall to his destruction. Is it not encoded in his genetic nature? Have not you made him so?"

"Before your oppression, he was not prone to faltering. He will fall, but he will not destroy himself. When provided the opportunity, he will choose freely. I have ordained it and you will not destroy him before he has chosen his path."

The Infinite Mind, by considering many factors, including subtle changes in thought, motivation, purpose, and circumstance, is able to foresee with precise accuracy far into the temporal boundary known to humans as time.

At times, the Infinite Mind will ordain a specific outcome and cause it to come about, either through direct intervention or by arranging a set of circumstances that are most conducive toward the results he desires. However, he always respects the dignity and free choice of every conscious being, even the Adversary's.

The Adversary spewed out a nakedly contemptuous retort. "He is nothing but a sentient organic creature with a temporary chemical existence—worthless talking dust."

* * * * * * *

In the dimension of time and space, Adam agonized in despair.

Chapter 13

Despair

Yosef's master took him, and put him into the prison,
a place where the king's prisoners were bound ... But
Adonai was with Yosef, and showed him mercy.
Beresheet 39:20–21

Adam would often utter the very same words spoken of him by the Adversary before the Tribunal, as if they had been whispered in his ears countless times throughout his life. Often, when looking at his image in a mirror, he would repeat, "I'm so worthless." These words reflected a profound self-hatred, a strange but common human reaction to abuse and oppression, especially if perpetrated while the humans were small children.

"You're a worthless misfit!"

He first heard the term "misfit" in an animated film about a mythical reindeer who had been rejected by his peers because of a notable and unique physical feature and then exiled to the Isle of Misfits. Adam wished there was such a place to which he could escape. Perhaps there, he thought, he would be accepted. He would not be ostracized there because, like everyone else, he would be a misfit in a world of misfits.

In reality, Adam was a misfit, that is, a nonconformist who did not fit the mold of what had become common human perspective and behavior. This was one of the factors involved in his selection as a fourth-generation bridge. But, his life was so painful, that at a very young age, Adam wished he could die or run away to anywhere he might fit in and be accepted.

Some of his most painful experiences occurred during his years in junior high school. The boy had a natural curiosity. He loved learning and school, at first. But around the age of twelve, when he first began to be shunned and punished relentlessly by other students, school became a place of torture - a living hell. Eventually, the mistreatment escalated to physical violence.

* * * * * * *

The Watchers had observed Adam struggling throughout his organic life. Their mode of observation was a strange phenomenon. At times, it was as if Adam had somehow been transported, in the flesh, to the Infinite Realm. But at other times, it was as if the Council convened in his dwelling, though never detected by him.

At one point during the proceeding in the Great Hall, when the Adversary petitioned for permission to destroy Adam, the Council appeared in his bedroom. The Advocate walked around Adam as he slept on his bed, and declared, "He is destined to prevail."

The Adversary, who also was present in Adam's bedroom, contended, "He lives in a deep sleep and does not even perceive you. As far as he is concerned, you do not even exist."

"You have sedated and blinded him, but I will open, am opening, have already opened his eyes."

The Adversary continued to argue, "But is he not guilty of transgressing nearly all of your universal laws? Will you not hold him accountable and uphold the standards you have established?"

"You have spoken truthfully. He is most certainly guilty of many transgressions, but he will be pardoned, is being pardoned, has been pardoned."

Perplexed, the Adversary responded, "Why do you plead for his cause? He is mere talking dust, decomposing organic matter, and unworthy of your attention."

"I declare him worthy," asserted the Infinite Mind. "He is the pinnacle of all created beings."

Upon hearing this, the Adversary shrieked in protest, "*I* am the pinnacle!"

"You once were the pinnacle of all created beings, but you allowed your heart to be darkened by evil. Hence, you forfeited your exalted position."

With obvious confusion, the Adversary responded, "He does not even care for himself. Why do you favor him so?" Seldom would the Adversary speak truth. He did so only when it served his purpose of manipulation. But in this case, he spoke accurately.

* * * * * * *

Adam did not love himself; on the contrary, he loathed his very being. Indeed, at the start of every frustrating day, at the end of each lonely night, and after each disappointment, he would often confirm the words of the Adversary: "I hate myself."

With angry self-contempt, Adam said these words when looking in a mirror or after having made a mistake. He despised himself, hating even the sound of his own name. In fact, he never hated or wanted to do violence to anyone but himself. Adam was drowning in a flood of despair, totally unaware that beings in another dimension would affect massive changes in his life and destiny by decree.

Chapter 14

The Decree

The sentence is rendered by decree of the Watchers.
—The Book of the Prophet Daniel 4:17

"He hates you!", the Adversary hissed vehemently.

The Adversary had deceived himself into believing that in the core of his being, the Infinite Mind was just as motivated by self-interest as he was. He believed self-interest was the essence of every being, and he intended to manipulate what he thought was the only possible vulnerability of the Infinite Mind. But the Infinite Mind, Adam's advocate, would not be manipulated.

Calmly, he responded, "How can he hate me? He does not even perceive me and so does not yet know me. You said so yourself. He hates only the perception you have created and injected into his mind."

The Infinite Mind continued, in the manner of communication common in the Infinite Realm when speaking of a time-transcending destiny. "Even if he were to hate me, I still favor, will favor, have favored the Man."

Persisting in his prosecution, the Adversary asserted, "He has disgraced you. He has spurned his potential and forfeited his right to life. He deserves death."

Surprisingly, the Infinite Mind now seemed to agree with him. "You have spoken accurately. He has forfeited his right to life, and his actions deserve the death penalty."

Upon hearing this, the Adversary was pleasantly surprised and thought he had finally succeeded in his prosecutorial endeavor. The rest was mere formality.

The Infinite Mind continued, "He is worthy of death. But, I give, will give, have given my life in exchange for his. You seek to destroy his organic life prematurely, and thus preempt his ability to enter the Infinite Realm. Judicial requirements demand that the Man suffer the death penalty. Therefore, in exchange for his life, I am entering, will enter, and have entered the space-time continuum and will assume, am assuming, and have already assumed an organic body that you will destroy, are destroying and have destroyed. In so doing, all judicial requirements of the Infinite Realm will be, are being, and have been satisfied."

The Adversary was utterly perplexed. He stammered, "Will you leave the Infinite Realm for a vile little human?" The Adversary could not conceive of any immortal being leaving the Infinite Realm of their own free will. He had been cast out and remained profoundly resentful.

"I am leaving, will leave, have left the Infinite Realm for the sake of the Man."

Still incredulous, the Adversary asked, "Will you truly relinquish your majesty for the sake of a mortal organic creature?"

"I have already done so."

The Adversary seethed with anger. He was sure a devious scheme was being concocted, a nefarious plot to nullify his rightful claim. It was a terribly unfair game. The Infinite Mind, who had created it, knew the end from the beginning. He knew every move his opponent was about to make. He could manipulate events and circumstances throughout all realities to elicit reactions most favorable to his ends.

The Adversary was exceptionally skillful at manipulating human thought and instigating the reactions he desired, but he could not control all events. He fumed as he reflected on this injustice.

He thought to himself, *"I am the greatest of all created conscious beings. Even the Infinite Mind affirms it."* But, the Adversary knew, deep beneath his arrogant shell, that he did not possess infinite intelligence. He wondered why, with his superlative powers, he could not be more like the Infinite Mind. He maintained that, as the architect of all realities, the Infinite Mind had constructed a labyrinth of possibilities with loopholes that allowed him to circumvent the very laws he had put in place, without technically breaking any of them.

The Adversary had once thought he could exalt himself to the level of the greatest being in existence, who sits on the Majestic Throne of all realities, but he had erred. He paid dearly for his arrogance and for following through on his self-deception. Humility, the quality of mind that enables a conscious being to accurately assess his strengths and deficiencies and then behave accordingly, was not built into his nature. He had to freely choose humility for it to become integrated into his character.

Most conscious beings either choose humility or develop it as a result of the mental distress associated with significant emotional experiences, such as major disappointments or failures. But the Adversary had no obvious flaws—or so he thought. Indeed, he had been created as a perfect being with no deficiencies and, before the Great Rebellion, had experienced no failures. The only distress he experienced resulted from his inability to have everything he wanted and thought he deserved—total and immediate freedom. He had no equals, and only one superior.

Frustrated, the Adversary protested, "He is my slave. I have already bound him."

The Infinite Mind responded,

"I DECLARE HIM FREE!"

This was not a mere declaration. It was an emphatic mandate uttered with authoritative finality. The Adversary knew it was a directive that would reverberate throughout all human history, proclaiming liberty not just for Adam, but for every person ever enslaved or held captive. Somehow, they would eventually be set free.

In that instant, despite temporal consequences, the eternal effects of all the malevolent designs of the Adversary and his claims upon the life of this human and all humans who were ever to come into existence were nullified in all realities in which they had been designed or were enacted. At that moment, inexorable changes were put in motion in the material universe and in all dimensions affecting the life of the man known on Earth as Adam, forever altering the trajectory of his life.

The Council that had convened in the realm outside time and space rose from their thrones. As with one powerful voice, a voice reverberating as the loud rolling thunder of a summer storm or rushing waters cascading from a mighty waterfall, the members of the Council shouted their decree.

"THE MAN IS FREE!"

Their thunderous words resounded,

"THE MAN IS FREE! THE MAN IS FREE! THE MAN IS FREE!"

Judgment had been rendered in favor of the man called Adam. Though unaware of it in the human realm, he had been granted freedom in the Infinite Realm.

Their words took the form of a beam of light going from the Infinite Realm through the Great Beyond, piercing through the observable universe. Proceeding relentlessly through the galaxy inhabited by humans, it went directly to the blue sphere called Earth with the singular purpose of liberating one specific human being who had been bound by perpetual oppression. By the decree of the Watchers, the man known as Adam had been set free.

At a precisely determined moment in Earth-time, by means of an inexplicable process, just as he had said he would, the Infinite Mind appeared in the space-time continuum as a mortal human being, subject to the inherent limits of a temporal existence and an organic body. This phenomenon was a profound mystery to humans. They could not comprehend that the Infinite Mind permeates and sustains every reality in existence. Every part of their universe existed within his consciousness and, as such, he could take on any form within that dimension at will.

Having taken the form of a mortal, the Infinite Mind willingly submitted to a torturous and undeserved execution in exchange for a human life. Many humans found this so inconceivable, that they relegated the account of these events to the domain of mythology. After the Infinite Mind assumed a mortal body, the Adversary unleashed all his fury against him and attempted to destroy him soon after the birth of his organic body. But his efforts were futile.

Still, the Adversary stalked him throughout his entire organic existence, subjecting him to nearly perpetual oppression and persecution. In human form, the Infinite Mind was despised and rejected by many, distrusted even by his peers and family members.

Eventually betrayed by a close associate, he was falsely accused, arrested, and sentenced to a brutal execution. The Adversary had inspired the creation of the most heinous form of execution known to man specifically to subject the Infinite Mind to a slow, torturous, and violent death. The Adversary had finally succeeded in striking a decisive blow and destroying the organic form of the Infinite Mind.

* * * * * * *

Suddenly, Adam's dream changed dramatically. It was no longer his other self on the scale, but someone else, another man. As Adam continued watching, he saw the man being brought before the tribunal. Once again, Adam heard the reading of a list of transgressions, of which the man on the scale was now being accused.

The prosecutor mentioned events at which and places where Adam remembered being present. He mentioned streets and neighborhoods that seemed strangely familiar to Adam. The prosecutor also referred to specific people Adam remembered being involved with. He felt as if the prosecutor was reading from the pages of his own life. Finally, Adam realized that it *was* his life the prosecutor was describing.

He was guilty of the offenses of which this other man was being accused. Never would he have imagined that some of the things he had done deserved a death penalty. Yet, here was someone in danger of losing his life for what Adam had done. Adam was completely helpless to do anything about it - not that he would have risked his own life by taking accountability for his actions. Even if Adam were willing to suffer the penalty he justly deserved, it would have been impossible to do so, because he was no longer an active participant. He was now a mere spectator, an audience of one, as if he were watching a movie all by himself.

As Adam watched, the man was offered an opportunity to speak in his own defense, but he refused. The prosecutor demanded of the man, "Have you nothing to say in your own defense?"

The man remained silent. The Adversary then launched an interminable assault, with accusation upon accusation, until it seemed to Adam that this man was being accused of every evil perpetrated by every human being who had ever lived. Adam recognized some of the transgressions of which the man was accused—historic evils spanning ages of human history, including war, oppression, and genocides.

The Adversary concluded his vehement denunciation with a derisive but somewhat hesitant, almost nervous laugh. He feared that a secret purpose was being played out, one he could not perceive. Was he being duped and used as a tool to further a process that might actually result in his own undoing?

He approached the man and whispered in his ear, "You have taken upon yourself every curse ever pronounced since the dawn of space-time, all for the sake of your pathetic organic creature."

Still the man said nothing. He stood silently-resolute and dignified, as if he knew that by willingly relinquishing his freedom and giving up his life, he was gaining a great victory. Adam wondered why the man would not defend himself. After all, unlike Adam, he was innocent of everything of which he was being accused.

The prosecutor concluded his argument with a closing remark that dripped with sarcasm, "Behold, *the man*."

A deafening silence followed this pronouncement lasting, what seemed to Adam, about half an Earth-hour.

Finally, one of the Watchers stood up and approached the white marble podium. A verdict was to be proclaimed. All the beings in the chamber focused intently on the Watcher standing at the podium. The previously brilliant hall dimmed and became almost completely dark. A blue light illuminated the Watcher at the podium, now holding the scroll containing the protocols of the Infinite Realm.

In a sober voice, the Watcher declared loudly, "He has assumed the man's guilt and accepted the penalty. Let the curse fall upon him."

The entire tribunal repeated, with one voice, "He has assumed the guilt and accepted the penalty. Let the curse fall upon him."

* * * * * * *

At that moment, Adam found himself on Earth. He heard a cacophony of haunting laughter and jeers erupting. It was the collective celebration of all the malevolent forces in the universe cheering together with one voice, as if they had won a great victory.

Adam saw men wearing robes that looked like garments worn during the period in human history then known as the first century. The man who had been accused of Adam's wrongdoings was condemned to death and then surrounded by a horde of executioners, who fell upon him like a pack of ravenous wolves. It was a horrific scene. The executioners seemed to take pleasure in torturing the man. They shrieked gleefully and derided him as they tore off chunks of his flesh. After brutally beating him, they impaled the man and left him to die a slow and excruciatingly painful death.

Appalled but unable to offer any help, Adam watched the man as he bled to death. Adam saw the man looking directly at him, just before taking his final labored breath. The man's face seemed familiar. Adam felt sure he had seen him before. He then realized the man had a striking resemblance to a being he had seen at the start of this bizarre experience. It was the being who had appeared in the Great Hall and said he would serve as Adam's advocate, when Adam had been brought before the tribunal.

As Adam witnessed the man's gruesome death, a preternatural darkness crept over the land. Adam felt the earth shaking violently, as if convulsing in an effort to expel the evil of injustice.

Then the scene changed again, and Adam saw the dead man's close friends and family members mourning for him. They took his body and prepared it for an honorable burial, according to first-century Near Eastern traditions.

Some of the conversation Adam overheard suggested that a great travesty of justice had just occurred. The man was totally innocent of the accusations against him, but he had been convicted and made to suffer a horrible execution.

Had someone else been punished and killed for what Adam had done? Had this man been executed in his place by mistake? Adam couldn't help thinking that this man's punishment should have been his own. But he was confused and wondered how that could be, since the man was apparently executed ages before Adam was even born.

These thoughts weighed heavily on Adam and settled deep within his consciousness. Then he felt something wet and warm dripping on his head and then running down his face. It ran down his chest and over his arms and legs, until he was completely covered by it. Adam looked at his hands and realized they were covered in blood. Somehow, he became completely covered by the innocent man's blood.

Adam wondered, *What could this possibly mean?* He then found himself standing at the end of a road that divided into two forks. One of the Luminous Beings he had seen in the tribunal appeared and approached him. This Watcher had a distinctly human appearance, although he glowed like all the other beings in the tribunal. He looked like an elderly man, though not at all frail.

With a perplexed look on his face, the Watcher asked Adam, "Why are you still here?"

"What do you mean, why am I still here?"

"You've been set free, yet you are still here."

"I didn't come here of my own accord. I was brought here against my will. I have no idea how I got here or how to get back home."

In very deliberate language, the Watcher responded: "He exchanged his life for yours. All judicial requirements have been met, and you have been pardoned of all charges. You have been set free."

"Are you saying that man died in my place? Why would he do that? Why would he give his life for mine? Who was he, anyway?"

"He gave his life to save yours, and to secure your freedom. Because of him, you are now free. Eventually, you will come to know who he is. He will guide you on a new path."

"How can he possibly do anything for me? He's dead. Isn't he?"

"Oh no, he is not dead. The death of the organic body he assumed cannot hold him. He is very much alive."

Adam asked, "Why was I brought here anyway? Why have I been shown these things?"

"You have been afforded a unique opportunity."

"What opportunity? Why?"

"You have been entrusted with the lives of many conscious organic beings. You are a bridge over which many of your kind will cross from bondage to freedom."

"Freedom? I don't understand," insisted Adam.

"In time, the veil over your eyes will be removed and you will understand," explained the Watcher. "You have a special destiny, but you must choose your path."

Still confused, Adam asked, "How can I choose a path if a destiny has already been designed for me? Isn't that a contradiction?"

"That is precisely what your Adversary wants you to believe. You can always choose your path. All free conscious beings must choose their own path—that is their universal right. You can choose to accept or reject your destiny."

Then the Watcher morphed into a horizontal streak of brilliant light and vanished. Adam thought about the Watcher's parting words as he contemplated the forked road before him. The path on the right led to a narrow trail going up toward a distant high mountain. The trail was rocky, thickly wooded, and seemed almost impassable. Adam could see that the trees prevented much sunlight from illuminating the path.

The other path seemed to be leading toward a beautiful lush valley. Adam felt inclined to take this path, but before he had taken a step, he heard the voice of the Watcher who had just appeared to him.

"Do not be fooled by illusions. Your organic mind is still shrouded by a veil. You have been traveling that path your entire organic life, and you know it well. It is the dark path. You will find that it will become increasingly darker as you continue on it. Walk long enough on it and you may not ever be able to find your way back. Go in peace. But take heed; the Adversary will seek to destroy you."

Adam was curious about this Adversary to whom the Watcher referred. Was he the prosecutor who came before the tribunal? Adam asked, "Who is this Adversary?"

The Watcher replied, "You will come to know him."

Adam felt a breeze blowing in the direction of the mountain path as the Watcher uttered his final words: "This is the way. Walk in it." Adam quickly turned toward the road leading to the mountain trail and began walking.

After a while, Adam sensed that he was being followed. Glancing back, he thought he saw a glowing figure trailing him. Adam became concerned and began to fear the worst. *What now?*, thought Adam. Was he a pawn in some cosmic game of cat and mouse? Were these beings toying with him?

Adam wondered if this nightmare would ever end. But then he remembered that the Watcher had told him he was free to go. He quickly ran off the trail into the thick woods in an attempt to avert the pursuing figure, though deep inside he knew there was no escaping these beings. He hid behind a large boulder for a few minutes, and then peered over it to see if he had succeeded in escaping. He was dismayed to see the being a short distance behind him, now holding a drawn sword. Adam's heart beat quickly as he watched the being, who was moving at a fast pace, come closer and closer to him. The being seemed to be running, but his feet were not touching the ground.

In an instant, he appeared right in front of Adam with his sword extended above Adam's head. Adam heard loud humming and crackling, as if the mysterious glowing sword was emitting electricity. He instinctively crouched in a fetal position, covered his face with his hands, and pleaded for mercy.

"Please don't kill me!"

Peering through his fingers, he saw the shining being wave his sword menacingly, but noticed the being was not looking at him. In fact, he seemed to be looking right through Adam. Turning around quickly, Adam saw a grotesque creature close behind him. Adam then realized that it was not he the glowing being was pursuing but the creature who had apparently been stalking Adam. The being quickly flew up above Adam's head and, waving his sword in a circular motion, drew a circle around Adam's body. An arc of bright light immediately encircled Adam, as if to warn the creature to come no closer.

Immediately the grotesque creature retreated and vanished. The glowing being also disappeared, but Adam suspected he was not alone. He proceeded cautiously on the mountain path, which seemed to be growing darker. Adam was afraid, unsure of his destination, and what else he might encounter on this journey.

Chapter 15

The Journey

Long before the birth of any conscious organic beings, the Infinite Mind led the Council of Watchers through a great labyrinth of possibilities. They explored thousands of possible life journeys for Adam and considered the potential ramifications of each one. The Infinite Mind knew each path intimately; he knew the eventual outcome, and which would yield the most favorable results in regard to Adam's destiny. The exploration was for the sake of the Watchers and helped define their individual journeys. It was then that a Guardian was appointed for Adam.

The Infinite Mind addressed Mikhael the Warrior. "Mikhael, you will remain with the man and see him safely through his organic sojourn, until it is time for him to enter Olam Habah."

"Yes, my lord," responded Mikhael.

Mikhael the Warrior knew no fear. He had successfully fought and prevailed against the Adversary during the Great Rebellion. He was prepared to, once again, do battle with any entity who challenged the authority of the Infinite Mind or threatened the peace of the Infinite Realm.

* * * * * *

Immediately after the Council of Watchers rendered judgment in Adam's favor, the Adversary vanished from the Great Hall. He appeared on Earth and stood with the Malevolence alongside Adam. But so did Adam's Guardian. The Adversary, enraged by the judgment rendered by the Council, had intended to unleash his fury upon Adam's mind and body. But Mikhael would shield Adam from the worst of the Adversary's attacks and ensure his survival.

The eve of Adam's awakening was one of the most dreadful nights he would ever endure. In the dark hours of the night, he awoke abruptly, in great distress from a bizarre and disturbing dream - the most vivid dream he had ever had. He remembered every detail clearly, as if he had been completely conscious. Adam recalled how, in some other dimension, his life had been hanging in the balance as he awaited judgment from a group of powerful alien beings. The most disturbing aspect of his dream was the fact that, after Adam was proven guilty by a merciless prosecutor, convicted and sentenced to death, someone else—an innocent man—voluntarily accepted the gruesome execution intended for Adam. As he watched him die, Adam was covered by the man's blood and then released.

Adam awoke from his dream shivering from a bone-chilling cold. It was unusually frigid in his apartment. He was breathing heavily, as if he had been running or exercising strenuously. When he turned on the light, he could see condensation from his breath. Adam wondered if something had gone wrong with the heating system.

An unnatural silence descended over Adam's dwelling. He could hear himself breathing. The air in Adam's apartment had grown heavy with the presence of the unseen Malevolence. Many powerful entities converged and began to engage frantically in a desperate effort to exert permanent control over Adam. The Lord of Melancholy, joined by the Entity of Self-Hatred, relentlessly assaulted his mind. He was then attacked by the Prince of Guilt and Shame.

Adam wrestled throughout the night with unseen forces of darkness. At first, he thought he was merely struggling with his usual anxiety about the issues in his life and the dark depression that perpetually clouded his mind and would often crush his spirit into hopeless submission. But this was different. After several hours, it seemed the worst was over. However, another struggle would soon ensue. It would be the most terrifying assault he would experience his entire life.

A profound fear descended over Adam like a deep freeze, chilling him to the marrow of his bones. For the first time in his life, he sensed an evil presence, someone or something, enter his dwelling-the dreadful Lord of Fear. This evil entity intended to fall upon Adam with an intense fury and coerce him to destroy his organic life. Adam was sweating profusely, but shivering with cold as if he had a fever. The malignant Lord seized Adam's nonmaterial self, the essence of his being, and clenched it in a viselike grip. Adam struggled to break free from his clutch but knew not how.

Adam's situation seemed hopeless. He felt he would surely lose control of his mind, and die alone and forgotten. Silently, he cried out for help in utter desperation. At that moment, Mikhael the Warrior arose and shielded Adam, with an invisible field, from the malevolent entities bent on his destruction. He caused Adam to descend into a deep sleep while he battled on his behalf.

* * * * * * *

Once again, Adam found himself in another dimension, suspended somewhere in the universe. He was witnessing a fierce battle being waged in the darkness of deep space by powerful beings. Adam was directly in front of a massive horde of grotesque creatures, very much like the creatures he had seen in his first dream, heading straight at him at an incredible speed. Suddenly a brilliant being appeared, holding a gleaming sword that seemed to emit energy, and stood directly between Adam and the approaching horde. With a wave of his hand, the being shielded Adam with a field of some sort. Adam realized he was the territory being fought over.

Mikhael, in a flaming body, wrestled alone with the malevolent entities seeking to destroy the man placed in his charge.

Adam heard horrific sounds; explosions, roaring, and frenzied shrieks. The hideous creatures hurled themselves at Adam, but were repelled by the protective field surrounding him. In a united effort, they attempted to attack Adam's protector. Mikhael unleashed the power of his lightning sword, an incomprehensibly powerful weapon of infinite power that only he could wield. He gripped the sword firmly with both hands as tremendous energy issued from it. With one blow, releasing more energy than the Earth's sun over many ages of time, he struck down the malevolent entities, leaving an arc of light where they had formerly stood to oppose him.

The attacking horde retreated instantly, shrieking and howling loudly as if in excruciating pain, then disappeared into the darkness of space. Mikhael emerged victorious.

* * * * * * *

Dawn of Light

The light of the morning sun finally awakened Adam. He felt exhausted after a disturbing and restless night, but he dragged himself out of bed. Barely awake, with sand in his eyes, he shuffled groggily to the bathroom. He never slept well these days and started every day under a thick, sleepy fog. Morning exhaustion was not a unique experience for him; morning had become the most oppressive part of his day. As he looked in the mirror, Adam knew the dark shadows under his eyes were more than just physical symptoms of chronic sleep deprivation. The previous night had been an unusual one, utterly different from any other he had ever experienced.

Adam stared at his reflection in the bathroom mirror. The first words that came to his mind were: "You look horrible." Strangely, the scathing self-criticism that went through Adam's mind now seemed to him as someone else's voice, as if someone else had taken up residence within him.

From that moment on, he felt as if there were two people living inside his body, two minds struggling against each other, each opposed to the other's values and intentions.

As he stared in the mirror, Adam couldn't help thinking that the tired and gaunt image he saw was not really him but someone else—someone he did not want to be. It looked and was dressed like him, but it was not him. It was someone else.

Adam sensed that something unusual had happened the previous night, but he did not realize that he had been the focus of a climactic confrontation between incredibly powerful forces. Evil entities bent on his destruction fought for control of Adam's mind, will, and freedom against a benevolent being charged with his protection. Adam had been allowed to see these two forces opposing each other in fierce battle, in a dimension outside time and space.

Few humans were ever aware of the unseen realities that affected their destiny. Similarly, Adam was unaware that, in another dimension, Watchers who were committed to guarding his freedom, had rendered judgment in his favor and, when necessary, would even alter the course of events in accordance with his destiny. Had he known this, he would not have started his day burdened with mundane cares; feeling stressed about going to work tired after a restless night. But, Adam would soon start awakening from the stupor in which he had spent his entire organic life.

The Guardian's mandate was to guide and protect Adam, and ensure his ability to freely choose or reject the destiny designed for him. He was not to be forced or coerced. Freedom is esteemed highly by the Infinite Realm. This was not the case with many humans, though some feigned love of freedom. During the Dark Time, the entire planet was held in bondage by the Malevolence. The Adversary had enslaved nearly all humans, many of whom, even while extolling the concept of liberty and fighting fiercely for their own personal freedom, denied the same to others.

For about six thousand Earth-years, humans sacrificed many lives on the altar of personal freedom. This was but one reflection of their unseen master, who fought vehemently for his own freedom while enslaving others.

Masquerades were hallmarks of the human world. Compulsions driven by unfulfilled needs were exalted as freedom of choice by some. Coerced choices born of dysfunction were seen by some as expressions of free will, whereas others decried them as crimes worthy of punishment.

Indeed, humans did have choices, but most of their choices were often harsh and dictated by others. Many of their alternatives were designed or corrupted by the Malevolence.

Few humans ever came to understand the power the forces of evil held over them or the oppression under which many of their kind labored as blind slaves to unseen masters. Oppressed by factors such as wars, violence, and abuse, many humans were compelled to choose between suffering for upholding justice and morality, or compromising their values in order to obtain relief from pain. Very few of them ever enjoyed true freedom in their world of illusions.

The Infinite Mind gave every conscious being an opportunity to exercise a truly free choice that would define their destiny. A choice of such import must be free; it cannot be coerced. Therefore, the Watchers rarely intervened directly in a way that would compromise a conscious being's free will. Their interventions mostly involved guiding certain events or creating skillful distractions, interrupting negative thought patterns long enough to promote a mind-set that would lead to a more positive result.

On two occasions, Adam's Guardian had to intervene at critical junctures to prevent Adam from destroying his own life. Suicide would not have been a free choice for Adam, nor was it his destiny. His life was meant to fulfill a specific purpose with a better destiny. When Adam was a young man in the depths of despair, he stood before a mirror with a blade in his hand, seriously contemplating suicide. He had thought about taking his own life many times, but never before did he have real intentions of acting upon those thoughts. Now, however, Adam had lost almost all hope. Words of encouragement, if they had been offered, could have done nothing for him that night. He desperately wanted the unending pain of his tortured life to end.

* * * * * *

The Watchers, who were continually observing Adam, detected his intention to harm himself. They instructed his Guardian, "Mikhael, alter his path. This will not be his destiny."

* * * * * *

On another occasion, when Adam was working on some tasks one evening, he decided to do two more things before going to bed. First, he wrote a last will and testament, which he folded, inserted in an envelope, and placed in his small file drawer. Then he wrote a letter he intended to mail the following day to his girlfriend, who was attending college in another state.

At the time, Adam was unaware that he was living with an underlying depression, a perpetual melancholy as if suffering a low-grade fever. His mind had become so weary from the continual oppression that he welcomed the idea of his death, and he began somewhat unconsciously, but methodically, preparing for it. Within a few days, he learned that the envelope he mailed to his girlfriend had not contained the letter he wrote to her, but the will that he thought he had filed away.

Upon receiving Adam's will, the young woman reacted with understandable alarm and assumed the worst—that Adam intended to take his own life. The young woman's reaction set off a chain of events that shocked Adam out of complacency. He was awakened to the reality that he actually had a death wish, and was shocked to see how close he had been to destroying himself and, in the process, hurting people who cared about him. Even more significantly, he realized there actually were people who cared whether he lived or died. This became a turning point in Adam's life.

The Watchers allowed Adam to descend to the depths of despair. But they had devised a plan that would enable him to ascend a height so great that it would later inspire others, that is, if he chose to fulfill his destiny.

* * * * * *

As the Adversary vanished from the Court in the Infinite Realm, so did the chains with which Adam had been bound. Unfortunately, for much of his organic life he remained unaware that he had been set free. Thus, began a long journey of discovery for Adam, during which time he never saw his Guardian or heard his voice, though his Guardian was always present.

In their world of illusions, what could not be sensed by humans was not considered real. Perception was their reality. Humans were only aware of what they could see, hear, taste, smell, feel, or measure. Hence, for many Earth-years, Adam remained totally unaware of being guided and protected, although later in life he began to sense his Guardian's constant presence by his side. Nevertheless, Adam was allowed to suffer consequences for wrong choices he made, as well as undeserved affliction resulting from evil perpetrated against him by others.

With the passing of time, Adam sensed that an unseen Guardian had snatched him from the gates of death several times, starting when he had fallen as an infant. When he was a young child, Adam's older brother had inadvertently lighted a blowtorch only inches from Adam's face. Much later in life, Adam considered this event and wondered why the torch had emitted gas but no flame into his face. He thought an accident of this nature should have been devastating, yet the gas did him no harm at all. Had it been a Guardian that had prevented Adam from being horribly disfigured or even killed or was it mere luck?

* * * * * *

In the Infinite Realm, the Watchers had observed this event and realized they would need to alter its outcome.

In another reality, they watched as the torch exploded into flames, engulfing the young boy's face and upper body. Adam survived after numerous surgeries, but remained blind and incapable of caring for himself. His face was not merely disfigured—it was completely erased. His eyes, nose, and mouth were seared closed and had to be reconstructed surgically, and his ears, hair, and eyebrows were gone.

That horrendous event resulted in a perpetual sense of loss, piercing loneliness, and profound despair for Adam. At the age of ten, he ended his own life, and eliminated the possibility of his destiny being fulfilled.

But in a dimension outside space and time, the Watchers decreed that events must be changed and created an alternative reality that allowed Adam an opportunity to choose his destiny.

* * * * * *

When Adam was only seven years old he was taken out of his house one night by a depraved man. The evildoer was a tool of the malevolent powers of the Dark Realm. Employed as a social worker, he had visited Adam's family earlier in the day on official business. He was a tall, clean-shaven young man with blond hair. Adam never forgot his deceptively friendly face and piercing blue eyes. The evil man was well dressed and wore a long trench coat, which he folded and draped over one arm as he entered the family's apartment.

That evening, Adam's parents went out and left the younger children in the care of the eldest son, who was about sixteen years old. That was the only time Adam could remember being left at home without at least one of his parents there. While Adam's parents were out, someone knocked on the door of the apartment. One of Adam's brothers opened the door and was surprised, but not suspicious, to see the social worker who had come to the house earlier that day.

The social worker explained to the brothers that he had been drafted to serve in the war in the country then known as Vietnam, and that he had to report for duty the next day. Years later, Adam still remembered seeing the official draft letter the man showed his brothers, complete with an embossed military seal, a subway token, and the date he was to report for duty. It was, indeed, the very next day. The social worker said that he had taken a liking to Adam and wanted to take him to the movies. His brothers thought Adam would be safe and decided to let him go.

The man took young Adam to a nearby theater. As soon as they sat down, he started to molest Adam and attempted to lure him to his apartment. Adam realized he was in horrible danger. He was terrified. *Why, he wondered, had he agreed to go with this man?* His heart pounded with fear. *Was he going to kill him?* Never had he been so afraid. He feared he might not be able to get back home, and also feared that if he made it home again, his father would beat him for leaving the house without permission.

* * * * * *

In another reality, one altered by the Watchers, Adam did not return home that night or ever. Thirty years later, the authorities finally discovered his remains and learned what horrible things had been done to the little boy known as Adam before his violent death at the hands of a depraved lunatic. The perpetrator had long since died, but the journal in which he recorded his evil deeds was found. He never faced justice during his organic life.

Had the Watchers not intervened and altered the course of events, Adam would not have lived long enough to fulfill his destiny.

* * * * * * *

The Watchers caused Adam to suddenly feel compelled to get up and leave the theater immediately. He followed his instinct, rose from his seat, and quickly walked out of the theater. The social worker remained in his seat and did not follow him.

It was night. Evil lurked and hovered around Adam like a dark cloud. But, after leaving the theatre, no Malevolent entity approached him, because an unseen Warrior walked by his side.

Adam concentrated so he wouldn't miss any landmarks and make a wrong turn. Cautiously, but quickly, he made a right turn out of the theater. He knew that at the next corner, he had to turn away from the clock tower he saw when he and his mother walked back from the department store. Adam walked safely through dangerous city streets and finally arrived at the five-story apartment building he called home.

He climbed the front stairs and stood in front of the building's heavy front door. Because of the criminal element in the neighborhood, as superintendent of the building, Adam's father had made sure there was a strong lock on the door and that it always remained locked, especially at night. Adam never remembered how he had managed to open the door.

Adam finally arrived at his family's apartment and timidly knocked on the door. His father opened the door without a word. Adam walked in cautiously; with great trepidation. He froze with fear when he saw the anger in his father's eyes. It was a look he knew only too well, a look that sent chills through him, because it nearly always foreshadowed a violent explosion.

Adam's father had already beaten his brothers for allowing him to go with the man. Adam was afraid he would be next, but his father did not hit him. In fact, he did not say a word to his son. Perhaps he realized Adam was just too young to know any better.

Although he was relieved not to be beaten, Adam was uncomfortable with his father's reaction. His youngest son, a boy only seven years old, had just arrived home safely after having been taken away at night by a stranger, yet Adam's father displayed no sense of relief. Anger was the only emotion Adam detected in his father when he arrived home that night. Adam was deeply hurt that his father showed no apparent concern about his safety and did not appear glad to see Adam arrive home safely.

For many years, Adam thought about the difference between the reactions of his father and his mother when he arrived home that night. His father never asked Adam what happened to him or if the man who took him had hurt him in any way. In sharp contrast, Adam's mother's response assured him that he was loved dearly by at least one person.

Almost immediately upon walking into their apartment that night, Adam saw his mother on the floor as if she had collapsed. Holding her head to her knees and crying inconsolably, she was desperately pleading for her young son to be protected and returned to her safely. She cried out in her native Spanish, *"Mi hijo, mi hijo! Ay, Dios mio, amparalo."* ["My son, my son! Oh, my God, protect him."] Adam's mother had never forgotten when she had nearly lost Adam, as an infant, to a premature death when he fell onto a concrete floor. She also remembered her neighbor's fervent conviction that their deity favored this child. When she saw her young son walk through the door, apparently unharmed, it was like seeing him come back from the grave a second time.

Still on her knees, Adam's mother was at eye level with her little boy. He looked into her face and saw the relief in her eyes as she burst into tears and embraced him tightly. She held him close and lavished him with love, as if trying to make sure he would never again leave her side. Meanwhile, Adam's father looked on angrily.

Adam's mother was thankful to see her son alive and well, but was unaware that an unseen Guardian, Mikhael the Warrior, had guided him home that night and delivered him safely to her. Later that night, as usual, Adam made the traditional request for his mother's blessing before going to bed. He felt guilty for causing his family such trouble, but was affected emotionally at a deep level by his mother's welcoming reaction upon his arrival that night. He longed to hear her comforting words. Adam prepared himself for bed, then went to his mother and quietly said, "Bendicion, Mami." ["Blessing, Mommy."] On Adam's native island, these words were traditionally spoken by many generations of children to their parents every day as they left or entered their home, and every night before going to bed.

Adam's mother blessed him with the same words she had always used: "Dios te bendiga y te Acompañe." ["May God bless you and keep you."] But she seemed to say the blessing with more tenderness and emotion than Adam had ever remembered.

Many years later, Adam would learn that these same words were part of an ancient priestly blessing, uttered for thousands of years over many generations. Though he did not realize it, just as his mother's blessing indicated, the Infinite Mind had been and would continue to be with him throughout his entire life.

Although knowing the boy could not hear him, Mikhael bowed on one knee and whispered to him, "You are greatly beloved, young master."

Indeed, he was.

Throughout his organic life, the Watchers protected Adam and steered him through many events, not all of which involved threats to his physical well-being, but all affected his destiny. When Adam had grown to manhood and was preparing for his upcoming marriage, he experienced the Watchers' intervention in different ways.

With only two weeks left until his wedding day, Adam and his fiancée had not yet found a suitable apartment. Time after time, they responded to advertisements for available apartments and showed up for their scheduled appointment, only to hear the owners say, "It's taken." Finally, one apartment owner made it clear in a telephone conversation that he would not rent to people of Adam's ethnicity, though he and his fiancée had stable jobs, good incomes, and excellent credit ratings. It was a most discouraging experience.

Adam had set August 15, two weeks before the wedding day, as his deadline for securing an apartment and circled the date on his calendar with a red marker. A few weeks before his deadline, he was shown an apartment on a quiet, tree-lined block directly across the street from a school. Although Adam and his fiancée both liked the apartment, the rent was more than they could comfortably afford. He was disappointed, but quickly moved on and put it out of his mind.

One night, exactly two weeks before his wedding, Adam went to see two more apartments and was yet again disappointed. Tired and frustrated when he arrived home, he had started to change from his work clothes and get ready to retire for the night when the phone rang. It was his real estate agent calling about the apartment Adam and his fiancée liked but thought they could not afford. She explained that the owner of the apartment liked Adam and his fiancée and was willing to lower the rent to meet their budget. Adam quickly got dressed, rushed over to meet the owner, and paid the necessary deposit.

Just before going to bed that night, Adam glanced at the calendar on his wall and noticed that the date, August 15, was circled boldly in red with a note that read: "Find apartment!" He had secured an apartment for himself and his fiancée on the exact deadline he had set. Adam laughed to himself, amused that events had somehow been altered for him at the very last minute.

He then remembered an incident that had taken place a few weeks earlier. Walking with a friend down a quiet, tree-lined block of brownstones, Adam mentioned how much he liked the area. As they passed a row of houses Adam liked, he pointed at a particular house and told his friend that when he got married, he'd like to live in a house "just like that one". Adam realized later that the apartment he had just put a deposit on was in the very same house to which he had pointed when walking with his friend several weeks before. By this point, Adam realized this was no mere coincidence, and he was pleasantly mystified by it.

Many years later, while driving home one Friday afternoon after a challenging week at work, feeling pleased that he had been able to leave work early, Adam was shocked to see a large truck coming from the opposite direction turning unexpectedly in front of his vehicle. Adam had just started crossing the intersection at a moderate speed, but the road was still wet just after a light winter's rain.

Adam tried to stop his car, but his wheels hydroplaned on the wet road. Still trying to avoid a collision, he turned the steering wheel sharply to the right, but his car continued on a straight path directly toward the truck. In a fraction of Earth-time, during which events seemed to move slowly, Adam thought of his wife and daughters and how his life was about to end. Sliding on the wet road, his car picked up speed as it headed directly toward the cab of the truck.

Upon impact, the truck's back tires rolled over the front of Adam's car. This resulted in much of the driver's side of the car being crushed, but it also prevented the car from going completely under the truck, which almost certainly would have resulted in decapitation. The car's front and rear windshields shattered, the airbag detonated, and the car became filled with smoke. Adam feared he would die engulfed in flames.

Thoughts, mostly in the form of impressions and feelings, raced through Adam's mind faster than he could express them with words. He knew he was going to die one day, but never thought it would be in a violent manner. He regretted that his family would receive a disturbing call later, but, strangely, he felt at peace.

But, as the truck rolled over his car, Adam was crushed under its wheels. His car exploded in flames and he was incinerated almost instantly.

****

In another dimension, the Watchers observed and altered that tragic reality, which was not to be Adam's destiny. His destiny was not to include a horrible premature death before his mission was accomplished.

****

In the alternate reality, fearing that his car could burst into flames any minute, Adam quickly attempted to open the driver's door, but it was jammed. His right hand was injured and he was unable to open the door with only his left hand, so he used his knee to push it open. The door finally creaked open enough to allow Adam to struggle out of the car, however, not being able to see out of any of the car's windows, he had no idea what he was walking into. He feared he might be struck by oncoming traffic, but he felt certain that staying inside the car would likely result in his death. Adam was able to walk out of the car safely, but with his face covered in blood from minor cuts on his head caused by shattered glass. Within a few minutes, he was taken to a hospital emergency room.

That night, while Adam was in the hospital under observation, the police officer on the scene visited him and told him in amazement, "The angels were with you tonight."

Mikhael whispered, in a voice inaudible to humans, "We are always with you."

Adam's Guardian had been with him that night, just as he had been with him every moment since the decree had been issued in Adam's favor in the unseen realm outside time and space. The Watchers prevented Adam from being crushed under the wheels of a 40,000-pound vehicle and delivered him safely home to his wife and children. Unfortunately, having no sensory perception of this awesome reality and weary of his journey, Adam still felt crushed in spirit. He desperately wanted to end the pain that had become chronic in his life. Rather than being inspired after having been protected from a gruesome death, Adam wished he had died in the accident. Besides pain in his marriage and stress in his family life, Adam still suffered some effects of the childhood abuse and the unrelenting oppression of the Malevolence he had endured. He also felt overwhelmed by crushing financial debt. Adam became despondent. He lost almost all hope and slipped steadily into a pattern of self-destructive behavior. He no longer considered suicide, but he stopped living and accepted an existence that was more of a slow death rather than life. He went back to the dark path.

* * * * * * *

In the dimension outside time and space, Mikhael, concerned about Adam's struggles, requested permission to alter Adam's journey so as to ease his suffering.

The Infinite Mind responded, "Let us consider the possible ramifications of a different path for the man."

Mikhael followed the Infinite Mind through a great labyrinth of alternate realities. They followed Adam through an alternate path in the space-time continuum.

It was a very different and much easier path from the one Adam had been on. In this reality, as a boy and then as a young man, he was more handsome, gregarious, and better favored by all, especially by women.

He was strong, athletic, skillful in sports, and successful in almost every endeavor he undertook. On this path, Adam developed great confidence in his abilities, but he also became proud and arrogant.

117

In many ways, he was a completely different person—selfish, self-centered, and shallow of heart and mind. He indulged in sensual pleasures and avoided introspection. He seldom had any concern for the plight of others who were less fortunate than himself. He took advantage of women, used them for his temporal sensual pleasure, and then left them to suffer the consequences on their own.

On this alternate path, Adam would adversely affect so many lives that much intervention would be needed to mitigate the effects of his self-centered lifestyle. In contrast, the actual path Adam was on, though at times painful, would result in positive impacts on many future generations of his family and indirect benefits for many others.

The Infinite Mind asked Mikhael, "If the Man were never to feel pain, how could he learn to appreciate comfort and be able to comfort others? Can an organic being who has never suffered or tasted the bitterness of injustice care to lift the arms of the weak or have compassion for the oppressed?"

Mikhael restated his concern, "My Lord, he sinks ever deeper into despair, and his attempts to escape his pain have spawned a cycle of dysfunction."

Ever patient, the Infinite Mind reassured him, "I will enable him to prevail over all obstacles."

"Can an organic being whose experiences are limited by space, time and their physical senses ever be truly capable of perceiving realities that transcend the boundaries of those limitations?" asked Mikhael.

"The embryo of eternity has been embedded in man's subconscious. However, though their organic eyes open at birth, humans remain asleep to infinite realities until they are awakened. Only when awakened, can they begin to perceive the essence of these realities and only then can they choose to embrace their destinies."

"Is there no alternate path that would yield a favorable result for the Man?"

The Infinite Mind responded gently, "Am I not intimately familiar with all possibilities? Am I not suffering, will I not suffer, have I not suffered with him? At the appointed time, I will provide him relief. I will weave every one of his experiences into a remarkable destiny. He shall be pressed but not crushed, and he will become a sanctuary for the oppressed."

* * * * * * *

Adam had been freed from the power of the Malevolence, but since he did not feel free, he remained unaware of his freedom for many years. Since the Watchers' decree, his hope had never failed, but it did falter at times. He experienced many opportunities and successes, but his emotional pain continued, and for many years he despaired as if he were still bound. Finally, after many Earth-years, Adam began to see the possibility of meaning and purpose in the suffering he had endured since childhood.

In the autumn of his life, Adam had another encounter with the Infinite Realm. He found himself again in that mysterious place to which he had been taken many years earlier, and just as before, he was bound and brought before the tribunal. Once again, he feared for his life. He waited with anticipation for the imposing being who had previously advocated for him, but he did not appear.

Just as before, formal charges were read. Adam was even more perplexed than during his first experience before the tribunal. Apparently, he was being accused of wrongfully imprisoning a conscious organic being against his will. Then, though no arguments were made in his defense, the entire tribunal vanished. Adam was left standing alone, suspended in dark blue space, holding on to bars in a cell in which he found himself imprisoned.

A Watcher appeared, the same being who had appeared as an elderly man and guided him onto a new path many years before. The Watcher asked Adam, "Why are you still here?"

Many years before, this same being had asked him the same question. Adam had not come to better understand the question since first hearing it and, therefore, he did not know how to respond.

"Sir, I still don't know what you mean by this question. I did not come here of my own accord. I was brought here somehow. What do I have to do to finally be free?"

"You are free. You were liberated long ago. You must now release *your* prisoner."

"What prisoner? I have no prisoners!"

"You stand within walls and hold on to bars that no longer exist. Release your prisoner."

Immediately Adam loosened his grip on the bars and let go, and they fell away from him. The bars then disappeared, along with the ceiling above him. For a moment, Adam was left standing on a platform floating in space and then instantly awoke back in his home on Earth.

In the course of time, Adam began to wonder if the purpose for his ordeal was somehow to help other people. As a young father with small children of his own, he once found himself holding the hand of a young woman he loved dearly. In deep despair, she had attempted to end her life.

Though their experiences were very different, Adam realized they had both been stalked and oppressed by the same malevolent entities bent on their destruction. Adam had never forgotten the painful time when he had considered ending his own life. That memory caused him to be moved with compassion for the young woman.

Later in his life, Adam befriended a young man who looked to him for compassion. Adam recognized the profound pain in the man's eyes. He knew it well. Like Adam, this young man had been oppressed by the Malevolence. Adam listened as the young man told him of the fierce battle he had waged within his own mind, trying desperately to hold on to his sanity, his dignity, and his sense of worth.

Though this young man was professionally successful and in excellent physical health, he suffered severely in the deepest recesses of his mind. Despised by his peers, he had often suffered abuse at their hands. As a teenager, he had been attacked and stabbed in the back of the head merely because he was different from those around him. His spirit suffered a more serious wound than his flesh.

Listening to the young man's story, Adam remembered when he had been surrounded and abused by a pack of aggressive boys. He identified with the painful humiliation he saw in this young man. Adam did not know what he could possibly say to encourage this young man. All he could do was listen compassionately and offer unwavering friendship.

Adam wondered if this was why he had suffered so much abuse and experienced such humiliating rejections. *Could it have all been to prepare him to help this person at this moment?*

He wondered if the purpose of his life could be to help others along on their path as they endured their particular experiences of suffering.

Adam was unaware that he had been advocated for in a tribunal convened in another dimension. Nevertheless, he began to slowly comprehend that in some mysterious way, he had been shown favor by the unseen powers that rule the universe. He began to believe that he had been offered a special destiny, though he was not yet sure what that could be.

Thousands of years before Adam was even born, his Advocate had assumed an organic life and willingly offered it as a sacrifice in exchange for Adam's life and freedom. Like most humans, Adam never understood that profound mystery.

Since childhood, he had read accounts of an inorganic, immortal being who, during ancient times, had descended to Earth and lived as a human. According to those accounts, this mysterious being, of his own free will, chose an incredibly painful path to fulfill a mission planned in another reality, a dimension outside time and space. This being willingly suffered a torturous death in exchange for the lives of the conscious organic beings known as humans.

For many years, Adam thought this account was a mere myth. How could atonement have been made for him before he even existed? But at one point, Adam began to think that perhaps, in some incomprehensible way, he had existed, long before his physical birth, within the consciousness of the infinite mind that created him. *Could it be that every human life had been similarly foreseen?*

Perhaps, Adam mused, he had been specifically advocated for even before he was born, not as one person among billions of others, but as one solitary individual, as singularly as he had entered the Earth and would, one day, depart. These musings arose from the seed of eternity embedded within Adam's human consciousness by the Infinite Mind.

As mortal beings, humans could not comprehend eternity, yet they were unable to imagine a reality without it. That is, they were unable to conceive of a reality in which they did not exist. Seldom would humans even have a dream in which they saw themselves die. As soon as they attempted to imagine a world in which they did not exist, they realized that, even as they thought about it, they continued to exist, if only as silent witnesses to events taking place in their minds. This reasoning also proceeded from the eternity seeded by the Infinite Mind in the heart of man.

Eventually, Adam came to believe that there was a purpose for everything he had experienced in his long, painful journey of discovery. Even his horrific experiences of childhood, though humiliating and painful, were designed to prepare him for a specific mission - though Adam was not certain what that mission would be.

* * * * * *

"Mikhael, how does the Man fare?" asked the Infinite Mind, though he knew the answer fully before Mikhael responded.

"My Lord, his spirit fares well, despite much emotional stress. He has developed great compassion for the oppressed and feels a natural desire to strengthen the arms of the feeble, just as you foresaw."

"You have done well, Mikhael. His journey on Earth must now come to an end."

* * * * * * *

Though it did not heal all the wounds Adam had suffered under the oppression of the Malevolence, the judgment pronounced in his favor in the Infinite Realm permanently secured his freedom. Adam had grown from boyhood to manhood and eventually became one of the aged ones. He took great pleasure in spending time with and reading to his beloved granddaughter.

One night, in the winter of his life, as he lay peacefully in his bed, Adam meditated on his life-journey and the lessons he had learned along the way. Because he had learned compassion, he had been able to help others with their particular life struggles. Despite much pain and disappointment, Adam had chosen life and found peace.

Adam never became important or influential, according to the standards of most of his fellow humans. Even at the end of his organic life, Adam felt he had not accomplished much. Few humans understood that performing acts of kindness and creating positive effects in the lives of others are great accomplishments that often transcend lifetimes. Adam's most remarkable achievement was that he had become a bridge that helped others to escape the grip of the Malevolence.

Occasionally, Adam would slip and fall to the bottom of the pit of despair he knew all too well, but the Watchers always lifted him out. By trying to relieve suffering wherever he could, he provided great inspiration and encouragement to others who had given up hope.

Adam's closest family members—his wife, children, and grandchildren—had gathered at his bedside. Sensing that his organic journey might soon be coming to an end, he thought about what parting gift he could bestow on his beloved youngest granddaughter. He motioned for her to come closer.

She leaned over and, as she had done as a young child when Adam read to her, rested her head on his chest. Adam placed his hands on her head and spoke some words in a language she did not understand.

"Y'va-reh-ch'cha Adonai v'yeesh-m'reh-cha, Ya-air Adonai pa-nahv ayleh-cha vee-choo-neh-ka, Yee-sa Adonai pa-nahv ay-leh-cha v'ya-same l'cha Shalom."

His granddaughter looked at him quizzically. "Grandpa, I don't understand what you said. What does that mean?"

Adam repeated the blessing in English: "May the LORD bless you and protect you. May the LORD smile on you and be gracious to you. May the LORD show you favor and give you peace."

* * * * * *

At that instant in Earth-time, a command uttered in the infinite dimension of the Watchers, was acted upon by two Guardians. "The mantle has been passed. Go swiftly to Earth! Stand by the child. You will guide and protect her from the Adversary and his Malevolence throughout her organic life."

* * * * * *

Immediately after Adam's blessing, a light shone all around his granddaughter. Two Luminous Beings appeared and stood on either side of the child. One was engulfed in flames and held a drawn sword. They were undetected by Adam and his family, but not by the Adversary, who stared intently at the young child. The meaning of this appearance was not lost on Mikhael. More than ever, he now understood, as the Adversary did also, how the destiny of the man he had been guarding transcended his organic life.

All along, the child had been the main focus of the plan. She had monumental importance. Adam was a bridge over which many conscious organic beings would cross from the dark path. She was to meet them on the other side and lead many on the path of light.

Once again, Adam thought about his life. It had been a long and difficult journey filled with much suffering, but also with much joy. Despite weaknesses he developed as a result of abuse and the work of the Malevolence, Adam never gave up hope. Neither did the Infinite Mind give up on Adam.

* * * * * * *

In the Infinite Realm, once again, words are spoken, will be spoken, were spoken about the man known as Adam.

"His has been a long and arduous Earth-journey. He has learned many lessons. He has developed compassion and helped many with their struggles. Despite many errors, much pain and disappointment, he has freely chosen life. His mission is complete."

* * * * * * *

Just before Adam finally closed his organic eyes to the human world, he heard an audible whisper, "Sleep, my friend. At the appointed time, we shall meet in Olam Habah."

Chapter 16

Olam Habah

Adam fell into a deep sleep but then immediately awoke, or so it seemed to him. In reality, many Earth-years had passed, but Adam was now in a timeless dimension and unaware of the passing of time. Opening his eyes, he found himself standing in front of a brilliant Luminous Being. Adam instantly recognized him as the one who advocated for him before the Tribunal in the Infinite Realm many years earlier. He wondered if he was dreaming again, but then he heard the booming voice and thundering echoes.

"No, my friend, you are not dreaming."

Though Adam had never actually seen this being or heard his voice, he realized he had known him for a long time. He now realized that this being had shadowed him his entire life, and he was filled with awe and gratitude.

In a softer voice, the being again spoke, "Adam, you have chosen well. You have accomplished your mission. Come. We have been waiting for you. All is prepared."

Adam trusted the speaker implicitly, but his curiosity prompted him to ask a question. "Sir, may I ask where you are taking me?"

"I am taking you to Olam Habah."

"Olam Habah? Where is that? What is it?"

"Where you will never again experience the bondage of evil or its effects. Freedom. I am taking you to freedom."

Adam knew they must have been traveling at an incredible speed and covering great distances. Curiously, after a while, it felt as if they were walking leisurely while everything moved around them. Then it seemed to Adam that they were standing perfectly still; suspended in space, watching the movement of the universe, as if it were putting on a pageant just for him.

Adam wondered if this is how nonorganic beings travel. "Perhaps", he mused, "they don't actually travel at all, but somehow appear where they choose to be. Fascinating." This was but the beginning of many wonders Adam was about to experience.

All of Adam's senses were awakened. As he approached what appeared to be a massive galaxy glowing against the darkest space he had ever seen, Adam actually felt, heard, and even tasted the vibrantly colored light emitted by the galaxy. As they entered the glowing lights, Adam saw what appeared to be a towering mountain, gleaming with brilliant light that illuminated an entire realm of lesser mountains, hills, fields, cities, massive oceans, rivers, and iridescent falls. Approaching the large mountain, they passed lower peaks and flew directly into an unbelievably beautiful sunset.

Adam's guide said, "These are the mountains of perpetual sunsets. They display whatever colors you wish to see."

As they flew higher toward the mountain, they passed iridescent waterfalls cascading out of lower peaks. The water glowed with vibrant hues of gold, yellow, and orange.

"You are seeing joy and exhilaration, which you often associated with what you called the color yellow."

For the first time in his life, Adam knew what yellow felt like. Amazed, he asked, "Is this an illusion?"

The Infinite Mind responded, "Are you an illusion? You and the entire universe in which you were born originated as a thought in the Infinite Mind. Every invention imagined and created by humans originated as mere thoughts. Were these illusions? You do not yet know what is real."

Adam couldn't help thinking that the most awesome wonders of the material universe now seemed to be mere reflections of the Infinite Realm, perhaps comparable to what humans called a movie trailer. Adam's guide continued, "In your organic life, you were always looking through a dark glass, longing for and anticipating the reality of a world you had never experienced and could not imagine, but somehow knew must exist."

They continued flying toward the top of the mountain and an immense city with gleaming white pearlescent walls. As they approached the center of the city, Adam saw a most incredible wonder. It was a massive sea that reminded Adam of a three-dimensional hologram, constantly alternating between what appeared to be crystal clear flowing water, glossy solid ice, and liquid glass.

An impressive platform, apparently carved out of highly polished white stone, stood in the middle of the sea. Leading to the top of the platform, on three sides, its left, right and front, were steps cut from what appeared to be massive diamonds.

Suddenly, Adam found himself walking alone and somewhat hesitantly on a walkway of flowing water that lead directly toward the platform. The surface of the watery walkway had the appearance of glistening crystal stonework. As he walked toward the platform, he was amused when he realized he was actually walking on water. He then saw the tribunal members sitting on twenty-four thrones arranged in a semi-circle around the base of the platform; twelve to his left and twelve to his right, and all facing him. An incredibly beautiful throne was set prominently in the center of the platform. The water which formed the walkway seemed to be flowing from under this throne.

The area around the throne was teeming with an incalculable multitude of beings, many of whom had human features. Crowds thronged both sides of the walkway, cheering, waving palms, and throwing garlands at Adam's feet. He wondered, "What is this all about?" The crowd seemed to be cheering for him and then, as with one voice, began loudly and enthusiastically chanting one word over and over again.

"FREEDOM! "FREEDOM! "FREEDOM!"

Adam recognized the warrior beings he had seen in dreams many years before, standing in formation on either side of the walkway with extended flaming swords forming a canopy above his head.

A Warrior who seemed very familiar to Adam waited at the base of the platform. As Adam approached, the Warrior lowered his sword to the ground, fell to one knee, and said, "I am Mikhael. I was your Guardian throughout your organic sojourn. Welcome, Master Adam."

Adam looked up and saw the being who had greeted him when he was awakened from death and guided him to this place. The being was standing before the throne at the top of the platform. As Adam looked intently on him, he recognized his face-it was the face of the man who had exchanged his life for Adam's when Adam was convicted and sentenced to death at his trial before the Tribunal. It was then that Adam realized that the man who gave his life for him was the same being who served as his Advocate during his trial. Adam was moved emotionally and instantly fell to his knees.

A glowing being approached the Advocate, holding a silk pillow on which rested a golden crown. The Advocate lifted a sword from a pedestal on his right, touched it to each of Adam's shoulders, and said, "You have chosen well, Adam. You chose to be a bridge over which many crossed from the dark path to light." The Advocate then took the crown and placed it on Adam's head.

"I am the Infinite Mind. Welcome to Olam Habah, my friend. Welcome to my realm. Welcome to freedom."

The Infinite Place

In a wondrous place
Transcending time and beyond space
Was freedom bought at an awesome price
By One whose life was sacrificed.

Through His demise and then His life,
Lowly men were made to rise.
The fearful had become the brave,
Nevermore to be enslaved.

Evil was forever banished,
Nevermore were any famished.
Firm stood he who once had stumbled,
For the arrogant had now been humbled.

Evil assailed,
But justice prevailed.

From darkest night,
Arose great light,
Brilliant rays
And endless days.

Epilogue

One thousand Earth-years had passed since the man called Adam was liberated from the clutches of the Adversary and the Malevolence. For one thousand revolutions of Earth around its sun, the entire planet and all humans were able to finally enjoy freedom from the once relentless oppression of the Evil One, the Adversary. He had been bound by a Warrior and placed in restraint. At long last, Earth and its inhabitants were free. Liberty was proclaimed throughout the land. The people who had dwelt in darkness were finally able to see the great light, which previously had been only dimly perceived by very few.

But then, for reasons known only to the Infinite Mind, the Adversary was released from restraint for a short season, whereupon he unleashed a new, short-lived but brutal, epoch of oppression and bondage.

* * * * * *

Once again, in the mysterious realm outside time and space, a tribunal convened in the Great Hall. The subject of the proceeding was a human who was guilty of many transgressions.

* * * * * *

The Woman was physically beautiful, but her spirit had been disfigured. She had been horribly and hopelessly oppressed, just as Adam had been. From her adolescence, the powers of darkness had worked to turn her physical beauty into a curse. Entities dedicated to the destruction of human dignity had dragged her into a pit of self-hatred, despair, and utter hopelessness.

One night as she cried, deeply depressed and in profound hopelessness, she decided to end her painful life. After writing a short note to her family, she took a sharp blade and stared at it for a few minutes, as if waiting for a revelation of some sort, a reason to continue living. She slipped into a deep sleep.

Though she had been chosen, just as Adam was, as an instrument to break the cycle of evil oppression over her family, she was blind to this purpose. She had not yet been given the opportunity to make a free choice that would define her eternal destiny.

The woman gave up trying to think of a reason to live. The more she thought about her life and the people she loved, the more she became convinced that she did not deserve to live. She put the blade to her wrist. She knew to make the incision parallel with her vein, not across it, to ensure the success of her suicide attempt. Though she trembled with fear, she placed the sharp point of the blade on her vein.

For a fleeting moment, she wondered if anyone anywhere in the universe cared about her. But that thought faded as quickly as it had appeared, and she set her mind again to her plan. She began to run the sharp point of the blade along her wrist, drawing a small amount of blood. She told herself that she had better do this quickly or she might change her mind. She lifted the blade and held it firmly in her hand, closed her eyes, and prepared to thrust it in and along her vein. Suddenly, while still holding the blade in her hand, the Woman fell into a profound sleep.

* * * * * *

In the Infinite Realm, the woman was brought before the tribunal. Once again, the Adversary acted as prosecutor, however, he no longer had personal access to the Infinite Realm. He addressed the Council remotely from his place of exile. The penalty he sought was death—eternal death. And as he had once done with Adam, the Adversary exhibited the woman in the most unfavorable light possible. She was utterly humiliated.

The Luminous Beings of the Tribunal took their places in the Great Hall.

The one who was once a human known as Adan de Las Aguas, now a highly-esteemed member of the Great Council, took his place in the Tribunal. He was now in a position to render judgment over the life and destiny of an unfortunate human being, one guilty of many transgressions just as he had once been.

In his prosecution, the Adversary proved beyond a shadow of a doubt that the woman was guilty of all charges and deserved the ultimate penalty.

He demanded a verdict consistent with the evidence.

"Is she not guilty? What is your judgment? Declare your judgment!"

* * * * * *

The Adversary pressed the Tribunal again for a response. "Declare your judgment!"

The Advocate appeared and declared, "You have no claim over her. I have already assumed her guilt and paid her penalty."

The once-man had not forgotten the compassion and undeserved favor once shown to him. As he had been forgiven much, he had come to love much. He addressed the Court. As had been spoken over him, he now spoke favor over one hopeless human being.

In unanimous agreement with the Infinite Mind, the once-man and the entire Council, declared,

"SHE IS FREE! SHE IS FREE! SHE IS FREE!"

Judgment was rendered in favor of the Woman and a decree was issued.

* * * * * *

As she slept, the Woman had a bizarre dream. In her dream, she found herself standing accused before a tribunal in another dimension. The evidence presented was incontrovertible and proved her guilt beyond a shadow of a doubt. She was guilty and worthy of the penalty, which was death.

However, before her sentencing, a curious turn of events transpired. An incredibly majestic being appeared and declared that he had already willingly accepted her punishment and paid the penalty she justly deserved. Then the judges unanimously ruled in her favor and declared her free.

A mysterious glowing being with the appearance of a young woman then approached her. The being said, "You have been pardoned. You are free. I will be your Guardian throughout your organic life. I have been in the darkness in which you were engulfed. I will walk with you and show you the way out. You, however, must choose to walk in it."

* * * * * *

Shortly after his last attempt to enslave humanity, the Adversary and his Malevolence were destroyed with eternal finality. Since then, all beings in all realities live forever free.

Printed in the United States
By Bookmasters